CRITICS RAVE FOR STEVEN TORRES AND *PRECINCT PUERTO RICO*!

"A most promising start to a new procedural series."
—*Library Journal* (Starred Review)

"A fine debut that will leave readers clamoring for an encore."
—*Booklist*

"A top-notch police procedural whose engrossing details create an authentic feel. Terse, deadpan prose, believable characters, and an offbeat setting add up to a promising series kickoff."
—*Kirkus Reviews* (Starred Review)

"Steven Torres has crafted a fascinating tale about illegal immigration and the clash between good and corrupt cops in Puerto Rico."
—José Latour, author of *Outcast*

"Steven Torres knows what he's doing. He has captured life on the edge of Puerto Rican society with a creepy realism that is consistently well-drawn, powerful, political, and which builds at a furious pace."
—K.j.a. Wishnia, Edgar-nominated author of *Red House*

GOOD ADVICE

Gonzalo pulled the photos out of their manila envelope and handed them one by one to Fernandez. He watched his deputy closely for a facial reaction, but Fernandez did nothing to hide his unease.

"These cops are from San Juan," Gonzalo pointed out.

"I know them. I'm here because I want nothing to do with them. Where'd you get these pictures?"

"Never mind where I got the pictures."

"The photographer'll be dead before he makes it off the island. If you talk to him again, tell him not to head for the airport."

"What do you mean?"

Fernandez sat on his bed and looked at the pictures even more closely.

"I mean these are bad people you have on film here. Walk away from them. Whatever they did, leave it be. Believe me. It's better that way."

PRECINCT
PUERTO RICO

STEVEN
TORRES

LEISURE BOOKS NEW YORK CITY·

A LEISURE BOOK®

July 2006

Published by

Dorchester Publishing Co., Inc.
200 Madison Avenue
New York, NY 10016

ISBN 0-8439-5734-4

Visit us on the web at www.dorchesterpub.com.

This book is dedicated to Damaris, my love,
Carmen and Esteban, my parents,
and to the many each year who do not
make it across the Mona Passage.

PRECINCT
PUERTO RICO

Chapter One

The beachfront town of Ramona, ten miles north of Punta Cana in the Dominican Republic, is one of the closest points on that island to American soil. Many inhabitants swear it takes only binoculars on a clear day to see the western coast of the island of Puerto Rico and freedom from economic despair. In fact, some say the binoculars are unneeded if one climbs a palm tree; with the sun at just the right angle, Puerto Rico appears as a spot of dark haze on the horizon. The image is an illusion, of course. Puerto Rico is a hundred miles away, and, if they see anything, it is one of the many tiny islands in the Mona Passage between the islands. They probably don't even see these.

The town itself is tiny if compared with New York or San Juan or any other city that would find its way onto a map. A row of shacks lines the beach. Another row of shacks lines up behind the first; another row behind that one and the town is complete. Is there a store? Certainly. Is there a vendor of cooked foods? Yes. Fried fish, baked clams, broiled crabmeat, Pepsi almost cold are all available in a small bodega/bar housed in one of the shacks on the beach. The store refuses to identify itself with a sign of any kind, and we won't impose upon it. Suffice to say that the only thing kept refrigerated is beer, and the most expensive items kept in stock are the fishing gear kept for the odd *gringo* who happens to stumble to this part of the island.

In this store, on this morning, two men sat at one of two small tables in close conversation. It was only just after dawn, but one of the men, in his forties but looking older and with three days' growth of stubble on his chin, had a half-finished beer bottle in his hand and a finished one sitting at his elbow. The other man was young and clean shaven; in fact, it appeared as though he had shaved only half an hour before, and he wore what may have been his neatest clothes—unlike his partner, his clothes were pressed and clean and he did not stink.

"So you understand what you have to do?" the drinker asked and raised the bottle to his lips waiting for a reply.

"Sure. I pilot the ship to Rincón. I go straight to

2

the lighthouse. I bring the ship as close to shore as I can, then everybody wades in. I guess I turn around when they are safe on land?"

"Why wait for that? If the Coast Guard is out, you'll have to drop them and go. The beach there is calm. Trust me. Just take them to the right of the lighthouse; hard right. Then go around to the left of it. I'll be there in a dinghy with a flashlight. Then you get the other half of your money. You understand?"

"Yeah. Nine. The last pier. Fourteen passengers, they all go belowdecks. Raul will be there to show me the way. I got it."

"Great. See how easy?"

"Yeah, but . . ."

"But what?"

"Are you sure you'll be there with the money?" The young man asked this in an even lower voice than he had been using.

The older man took the bottle from his lips slowly.

"Let me ask you a question. Didn't you come to me looking for this job? Didn't you say you needed the work? You needed the money. I'm trusting you with the ship. You should trust me with the money, okay? Now don't talk about it again. There are a lot of guys on this island who would do this for a lot less."

The young man was ashamed he had asked the

question and afraid because he knew how easily he could be replaced. The drinker finished his beer, staring at the young man all the while.

"What kind of experience did you say you had?" he asked.

"I was with the Coastal Patrol for six years. I then went into fishing with my father. I did this for two years. But my father died. My uncle inherited the boat, and he has three sons. I work for him from time to time, but only when he pities me. I'm good at this. I can pilot a larger ship than this."

There was pride in the way he said all this, and the older man looked at him more closely. He wondered if any of what he heard was based in truth. He had hired a dozen men for this type of job over the years. All of them said they had been in the navy or Coastal Patrol or captains of their own ships. After they got to the ship, they all needed to be told how to turn the engines on; they all needed just a few pointers on how to steer the vessel. One had even spent five minutes revving the engine, trying to pull away from the dock without having untied the ship. This one seemed like he might actually know how to pilot the ship and so he watched him until the young man became nervous.

"What?" he asked.

"Oh, nothing," the older man answered. "Just

be there at nine. The last dock. Raul will give you the first half of the money and whatever instructions you need. Now go to sleep. It will be a long night for you."

The young man got up and gave the table a sharp rap with his knuckles, making the same sound an auctioneer uses to conclude a sale or a judge does upon pronouncing sentence. What had been sold at that moment, what the penalty was, remained to be seen. The young man walked out. The other man ordered a third beer.

For the young man, home was one of the shacks a hundred yards inland from the beach. The one room was large but spare, though it contained all he had in the world. When he walked in, his infant daughter was sleeping soundly in a worn-out crib in one corner of the home; his wife was making coffee. Normally he would have come up from behind her to embrace her, but he felt ashamed of what he was about to do. He knew the American government opposed people who crossed their borders. In fact, he was sure they considered the smuggling he was about to undertake a crime. He wondered what his government thought of the issue. His guess was that they didn't think of it at all. Probably they were glad to be rid of a few hungry mouths. Still, though he was about to do a service for his country, he didn't feel like holding his wife.

He threw himself into a hammock and used a foot to rock himself gently.

"Did you get any work?" his wife asked.

There was no intent to pressure him with these words. If he had just come in from work, she would have asked how his day was in just the same tone. But in some men, the best men, any reminder of their joblessness is a painful thorn in their heel. Today he had an answer.

"I'm going in to work tonight—deep-water fishing," he said, laying his forearm across his eyes.

"How deep?" she asked.

"Listen, Isabel. I haven't worked in more than three weeks and that last job didn't do anything for my pocket. I'm working for an *Americano* . . ." he lied. "He said he would pay me twenty dollars for every hour. Twenty *American* dollars. If he wants me to take him to Africa, that's where we're going."

Isabel was quiet for a moment and brought his coffee.

"How long will you be gone?"

"Well, I don't know, but I think I should be back by tomorrow night or the next morning at the latest. If it's going to be later than that, I'll try to radio someone to get in touch with you, okay?"

"Don't worry about me, Marcos. Worry about yourself. Take care of yourself. Sometimes *Americanos* promise a lot but don't pay."

Marcos held up a hand.

"Don't even think about that. This one has money. He's going to give me some before we leave. He said two hundred and fifty American dollars up front. If I get a chance, I'll bring it over before we go out to sea."

"Good. We can use the money."

"Well, don't hold your breath. If he's in a hurry, you won't see anything for a day or two, you understand?"

"We can hold out until then," Isabel answered.

"Good."

Marcos slept in fits until six that night. He rose from the hammock less rested than when he had lain down. He dressed in his best clothes, a white shirt and beige pants he wore to church. He shaved again though the hair on his face had hardly had time to emerge from his skin. He ate a simple dinner of local viands and codfish, then left the house after pacing nervously until eight.

"But you'll be very early," Isabel pointed out.

"That's good. If there's anyone there they might be able to pay me something and give me time to get the money to you."

With a kiss for his wife and one for his daughter, he left the shack and walked briskly the few hundred yards to the last dock on the beachfront. He was nervous and wanted to work off some of his excess energy before meeting Raul.

Raul was short and skinny with dirty, sweat-stained clothes. There was a greased baseball cap on his head, and his shirt was open to the navel. The bones of his chest were plainly visible. He waved to Marcos as he approached, and Marcos stepped to him and shook his hand firmly.

"You're early," Raul said.

"Your *jefe* said he would leave some money with you for me. I was hoping—"

Raul held up a hand and reached into a rear pant pocket.

"*Toma.* Here it is." Raul handed Marcos a dirty, sealed envelope.

Inside the envelope there was fifty dollars and a note of explanation:

Marcos,
   I had to get back to Puerto Rico. It was an emergency. I owe you $450. Don't worry. You'll be paid when you meet me over there. Take care of the ship.

Marcos burned. He was expecting another two hundred dollars in the envelope. Fifty American dollars were substantial, but they were not a trophy to bring home to his wife. He felt embarrassed and shoved the money into his pocket.

"Is something wrong?" Raul asked, though Marcos couldn't help thinking the shriveled little man was part of the deception.

"I was expecting more in the envelope," Marcos said as coolly as he could.

"Oh. I don't know what to say. I have five dollars. Does that help? *El jefe* will pay me back. But, hey, if he doesn't pay you, you can always keep the boat."

The old man held out a crumpled five-dollar bill.

"Forget about it. Let's just get to work. Where's the ship?"

"Right here. Don't tell me you're blind." Marcos looked around. There was a ship right next to him, but it wasn't the beautiful, new ship he had been shown in the morning.

"What's this?" he asked.

"That's it. *El jefe* said he had shown you the boat." The little man took off his greasy cap and scratched his greasy hair.

"He showed me a boat this morning, but not this old thing," Marcos replied.

"Oh. He probably showed you *La Princesa*— that's his boat—I mean for his own use. This he just uses once in a while. It's bigger. There are a few more passengers. He said you told him you could handle a bigger boat—"

"Then he has to pay more money."

"That I don't know about. You have to speak to *el jefe* about that. Still, this is a good boat."

"It doesn't look so great."

"Ah, but the engine is the heart of the boat. The

9

heart. I fixed it myself. Get in; turn it on; see for yourself."

The little man gave Marcos a nudge towards the boat with a filthy elbow.

Marcos climbed aboard and went to the helm. Every instrument, every gauge and knob was cracked and dirty except for a few that were missing altogether. The fuel gauge read full, which was a relief. The captain's chair was torn and wobbly when he sat in it. He brought both hands to his face. He could hardly believe he was about to take the boat out into deep water when he did not feel safe while it was tied to the dock.

"It's a good ship if you treat her right. It'll get you across to Puerto Rico and back without a problem, I guarantee it as a man. On my mother's grave I tell you this."

"I'm gonna do it no matter what. I need the work."

"That's the way to think about it. Now, since you're already here, why don't you just rev her up a little and take her out now; it'll get you home a little earlier."

Marcos laughed.

"Shouldn't I wait for the people?" he asked.

"What people?"

"The passengers."

"They're already locked up belowdecks."

The little man hopped down to the hatch leading belowdecks, took a padlock off and opened it. A hand shot up and clutched at the deck. The little man stepped on it, and it was pulled back.

"Todavía no," he said. "Not yet."

From the quick glimpse into the hull, Marcos saw parts of about eight or nine people huddled closely together.

"How many are down there?" he demanded.

Raul squinted up toward the sky.

"Twenty-two?" he asked as though Marcos had a better idea.

"Twenty-two?" Marcos repeated. "How many people does this ship hold?"

"What do you mean? Legally?" Raul answered.

"Forget it. Let me get out of here. The ship is stocked with all the safety equipment I need?"

"Like what?" Raul asked.

"Life jackets, for instance."

"Sure. Here's yours."

Raul got a life jacket from a locker near the captain's chair and presented it to Marcos.

"What about the others?" Marcos asked.

"Who?"

Marcos pointed at the hatch.

"Them? Don't worry about them. They have jackets."

"Can I see?"

"Better if you don't open the hatch until you get to Puerto Rico. Some of them get drunk. Some of

11

them get afraid. If they get out of there, you'll never be able to control them. Trust me. Keep the lock on the hatch until you get near the lighthouse, then let them swim to shore. Believe me. I've done this a dozen times. Now get going. You were here early, but it's almost nine now."

Raul made his way back to the dock as Marcos primed the engine. It didn't sound bad at all, which was a relief, and he couldn't see belowdecks where a half-cup of water filtered through the hull as soon as the ship hit its first wave.

A few minutes later, as the boat entered the open waters of the Caribbean, Marcos looked back towards the town of Ramona. He wondered if any of the lights now growing dim were the lights of his home. He wondered if his Isabel was looking back at him at that moment, and he raised his hand to wave just in case. He had never left home before with so many fears, so he quickly turned his back on his home and stared out to sea toward Puerto Rico. He never touched either shore alive again.

Chapter Two

It wasn't that he was opposed to change. Luis Gonzalo, the sheriff of Angustias, often welcomed it.

When his budget was increased and he was told his force was going to be doubled with three new officers, he was ecstatic. When the mayor of Angustias explained with some trepidation that the government of Puerto Rico was now going to require that they install a computer with a modem, that they needed to get a "fats" machine, Gonzalo was a little wary but not unwilling to believe the gadgets might help. It was 1987, and he knew the drug dealers, the *sin vergüenzas* who had only recently found Angustias on their map, had high-tech equipment. If it was good for them, he wanted to know how it worked.

But everyone knew he drew the line at remodeling and enlarging the station house. With only one cell, with room for only two desks, there was a desperate need for more space. He had resisted this change for a dozen years. On this particular issue, he could not be made to see reason; all he could see was that an expansion of the existing facilities meant tearing down walls and interrupting his work. This, he could not accept, so this time he was not given the choice. When he came in to work shortly before noon on the first Thursday in February, there was a wall already made into rubble, sitting in the back of a dump truck.

Gonzalo controlled his first impulse. He wanted to rush at the workers, to make them stop. He wanted to demand to know who ordered this . . . this abomination. Actually, for a moment perhaps too short to be worthy of note, he wanted to take out his gun and start shooting indiscriminately. He repressed all these feelings. Instead he folded his arms across his chest and leaned back against his car, staring at the workers removing bits of debris that used to be the wall where his bulletin board had hung for nearly two dozen years.

There were ten men with twenty eyes, and not a single worker could spare Gonzalo a glance. When he found his gaze could not wither them or stop them or make them disappear, he walked past them and into what was left of the station house.

Inside, two of his deputies were sitting on one of the desks that had been pushed up against the far wall.

"Where are the chairs?" he yelled over the noise of a hand-held jackhammer someone had just turned on.

Both deputies pointed to the cell at the back of the building. In it were the four chairs and two file cabinets that more or less rounded out the office furnishings. These were piled up against the rear wall. Both side walls had gaping holes where iron bars had once prevented escape through windows.

"Who did that?" he asked.

"The workers," Deputy Pareda answered.

Gonzalo thought a minute.

"There were no prisoners in there, I hope."

"Nah, we let 'em go before the work started."

Gonzalo looked at Pareda.

"I'm serious," Pareda protested. "There were two drunks. Collazo arrested them last night. They were almost sober this morning, so I gave them tickets and sent them home."

Gonzalo turned to look at the work from the inside of the station house. He thought he might have handled the prisoner situation differently, but these were extraordinary circumstances and letting them go with tickets was within the range of options. There was no need to question Pareda about this decision.

"Let's go outside," he told his deputies and they followed him out the front door.

Outside was warm. The sky had reached a deep, rich blue that has not yet been found on any painter's palette. Gonzalo squinted up at the sound of a small hawk indigenous to the island. As is often the case, the bird was being run off by a pair of hummingbirds. Gonzalo wondered how many generations this battle had been raging and what was the initial cause.

"Officer Calderon, you spent your first three days of service with us figuring out the new computers, determining what they could do for us. I read your preliminary report last night, and I was impressed."

"Well, computers are the wave of the future, sir," she responded.

"I was impressed by the thoroughness of your report; I'm still a skeptic about the machines themselves. I was going to ask you to help me get some hands-on experience on the thing today, but obviously that will have to wait. . . ."

"Officer Pareda had suggested that he could drive me around the town to help me familiarize myself with the landmarks, the roads, the people . . ."

"That's just what I was going to suggest, but with one slight change. Officer Pareda should be the passenger."

"But—" Pareda began.

"No buts. I don't need you giving Officer Calderon a tour of Angustias at eighty miles an hour."

"But—"

"Just do what I say, Hector. Okay?"

Hector was twenty-seven years old, but he sometimes approached life with a startling immaturity. Gonzalo accepted this because after all, Hector was a good worker, a brave officer, young and handsome, and in the end he did as asked without fail.

The two officers climbed into the only squad car.

"Be back in an hour," Gonzalo ordered, but he wasn't sure he was heard above the noise of construction.

In the passenger seat of the squad car, Hector Pareda found himself with little to do for a while but look at his partner closely. Iris Calderon wasn't particularly beautiful, he decided. She wore her hair at shoulder length, and he preferred women's hair much longer. She was tall for a woman, but thin; lanky almost. He preferred a fuller figure in a woman. Her lips were a little

17

thinner, her face a little paler than he liked. In fact, he didn't know why he was following this train of thought at all. He was currently infatuated with the sheriff of Naranjito, and she was everything he had ever wanted in a woman—except receptive of his subtle advances. He turned to face forward.

"Got tired of looking me over?" Officer Calderon asked. She turned to him for a moment with her lips curled into a smile that Hector was certain had some asymmetry to it.

"I wasn't looking at you," Hector lied.

"Really? I'm hurt," she said with a pout that was similarly asymmetrical. It made Hector nervous.

"I mean, I was looking at you, but not with any romantic intentions. That doesn't sound so good. I mean I was looking at you but in the same way I would look at a guy—"

"Is that supposed to sound better, Officer Pareda?"

"Turn left here. Call me Hector. Look. I was looking at you. I just didn't mean you any harm. You don't have anything to fear from me."

"Hector, when I graduated from the academy, they gave me a gun, a can of mace, and told me my partner was my friend. I wasn't afraid of you. Come on, loosen up a little."

"I'm loose. In fact, of all the officers who protect and serve in Puerto Rico, there isn't a looser one than me. Stop right here."

The officers got out of the car in front of a narrow walkway that led into thick underbrush and over a short rise.

"Where are we going?" Calderon asked while following Hector along the trail, but he ignored her.

The path sloped gently down the other side of the rise and opened into an overgrown grassy clearing with a wooden shack standing on four cement pilings. The officers walked up to the front door, which was left entirely open. Inside there was almost nothing—a few pictures on the wall, two chairs, a small table, and a hammock with both ends hanging on one hook. On a small shelf attached to the wall, there was a portable radio.

"Doña Carmen," Hector called out, though he couldn't explain to himself why—she clearly wasn't in the room.

"*¿Qué quieres?*" came a response from somewhere in the bushes to the side of the house.

Doña Carmen emerged from the woods near her home carrying a metal pail near brimful with water. She was just then entering her eighties with a brown skin so thin, so sharply wrinkled, it almost seemed possible to peel it off without hurting her, as one might remove the shell from a hard-boiled egg. While she was robust for her years, she was a small woman, and the pail seemed to tax her strength. Hector rushed forward to take the bucket from her.

"What happened to the hose I set up?" Hector asked as he brought the pail into the house.

"*Ay, mi'jo*. It takes too much energy to pump the tank full. All I want is a little bit of water to wash a few dishes and make a proper breakfast."

"Doña Carmen. It takes ten minutes to pump fifty gallons—"

"It takes you ten minutes. I'm an old woman. *Papa Dios* is going to come for me soon, what do I want fifty gallons for?" She smiled.

"Nonsense. You've been talking about *Papa Dios* for a dozen years now. He forgot you. Look. I'll go hook up the hose and fill the tank. What I really came here for was for you to tell our new deputy here, Deputy Calderon, the same thing you told me when I first started as an officer."

"What did I say?" Doña Carmen asked, truly befuddled.

Hector wagged his finger at her. "Those words of yours changed my whole outlook on life. They made me the officer I am today. Don't be modest. I'll be back in a few minutes," he said. Then he left.

Doña Carmen sat down on one of the chairs in the room, and after a moment of reflection, she motioned Officer Calderon into the other chair with a weak smile. The conversation Hector was referring to had taken place seven years earlier, and while she loved Hector like a grandson, she was a bit upset with him for presuming that she had memorized every word that had passed between them.

"Want coffee?" she asked the deputy.

"No, no. Don't trouble yourself."

It was clear to Calderon that Doña Carmen had forgotten the words of wisdom she had given Hector some years earlier. It gave the officer some slight pain to know the old woman was racking her brains for a scrap of information that was no longer there, but Iris could not think of a way of putting Doña Carmen at her ease. After a minute more Doña Carmen broached the subject herself.

"I don't know what I told him that made him a better policeman," Carmen said, straining to recall. "I never was a policeman myself," she hurried to explain, as though to dispel an ill-founded rumor.

There was a moment or two more of awkward stillness in the room.

"I'll tell you though, one thing can be learned from this little episode. Maybe you can use it in life—the things you say and do, no matter how unimportant you think they are, can be very important to the people around you. I said something to Hector, I don't even know what, but he took it to heart. As my grandmother used to say—'Even the leaf that falls is important to the bird building a nest.' "

The two women sat in silence a minute more and when Hector returned, he bowed to the old woman in her seat. She put an arm around his neck and kissed his check.

"Que Dios y La Virgen te acompañe y te cuide," she said. *May God and the Virgin be with you and protect you.*

Hector and Iris went on to visit several other members of the community that hour, but he could not get from his junior partner what wisdom Doña Carmen had given her. Iris would not discuss it for fear of revealing the old woman's frail memory. Little did she know Doña Carmen had said essentially the same words to Hector when Gonzalo had brought him over. The sheriff of Angustias had also asked that she repeat the words given to him fifteen years earlier when he had become the first sheriff of the small town.

While Hector and Iris were busy at Doña Carmen's house, Gonzalo was trying for the fourth time that week to warm up to Abel Fernandez, the new deputy he had given himself as a protégé. At thirty-five, Abel was the oldest and most experienced of the three new deputies, and Gonzalo had hoped that this would make the transition into the new precinct a relatively easy one, but Abel was set in his ways and had picked up a variety of bad habits. These included taking a longer-than-usual lunch and turning the radio down while he was eating.

Abel rarely acknowledged the looks cast upon him by others and never smiled or waved. Even when he spoke to Gonzalo he seemed to be suffering from the exchange. Gonzalo was sure his deputy would go through the day without speaking to a soul if he could, and he wasn't too sure Abel wouldn't just pack up and go home if he weren't watched. After several days of working together, the sheriff of Angustias felt he had gotten nowhere in solving the riddle presented by his own deputy, and, frankly, the situation annoyed him a little.

Gonzalo met Abel outside the station house as the deputy came to report to work. Gonzalo motioned for Abel to walk with him towards the town plaza. Gonzalo began the conversation with talk of the weather. It was the rainy season for that part of Puerto Rico, but Angustias had not seen a drop in nearly a month. The sheriff then turned his attention to winter league baseball. Neither of these topics seemed to be of interest to Abel, and there were long pauses where the two men simply stood next to each other. At the end of one of these pauses, Gonzalo decided to steer conversation subtly towards Abel's disturbing detachment.

"So, Abel, I thought today we might pass by the

elementary school when it lets out and talk with some of the children as they wait for the bus."

Gonzalo ended his sentence with a note of expectation—he expected his deputy to have a response to this suggestion, but Abel just shrugged.

"Until then, I was thinking you should get acquainted with the clinic and the people who work there. We work with them on all sorts of things, and they're good people."

Abel didn't even shrug at this idea.

"Look. You transferred from San Juan. You asked to come out here. I know it can be difficult. Angustias is no San Juan. We are a small town with little excitement, but the people can be very nice once they get to know you. You have to give them a chance."

"Did I say I wasn't going to give them a chance?"

"But you're not giving them a chance. You show no interest in anybody in town—"

"I don't know anybody in town."

"Exactly, and it looks like you don't really want to know anyone."

Abel shrugged at this suggestion as well. He squinted toward the noon sun, then toward the plaza fountain. The relic gurgled on without a care for the deputy's problems. He searched the trees that lined the plaza and the façade of the church at the far end of the promenade—none of these had an answer for him.

"I don't know what to say," the deputy said finally. "I'll try to do better. I don't mean to appear unsociable—it's just an attitude I picked up from working in San Juan, I guess."

"Okay, but just remember, this isn't San Juan, okay?"

"Sure," Abel answered, and at that moment Hector and Iris brought back the squad car.

It did not dawn on the sheriff that the differences he perceived between the big city and this tiny *pueblito* of nine thousand or so were not the same as those Abel understood. While Abel saw Angustias as a place to hide from the pressure of having to interact with hundreds or thousands, Gonzalo knew the truth of small town life: there was no privacy, no place to hide from anyone. There wasn't an anonymous soul in all of Angustias.

Their shift was over at eight o'clock, but Gonzalo asked Abel to put in extra hours during the first week to familiarize himself with the people and the rhythms of the town. By midnight, however, Abel had left and Gonzalo started home for what he hoped would be a restful evening.

Deputy Emilio Collazo was left to spend the night with his young trainee, Rosa Almodovar, in the three-walled station house. A blue tarp was bolted snugly to cover the missing wall. The officers made extremely small talk for an hour before Collazo exhausted his social skills and Rosa began to lose her patience. Then the phone rang.

"Uh-huh. Uh-huh." Collazo looked up from his desk, a phone stuck to his ear, a look of complete exasperation scratched onto his face.

"Uh-huh," he said, one more time; then he put his hand over the receiver.

"Do you speak English?" he asked his new partner.

"Sure," she replied.

"Good. Talk to this *gringo*. I don't know what he wants from me."

Deputy Almodovar took the phone from Collazo and began jabbering. Collazo, now well over seventy, was fascinated by the stop and go rhythm flowing from the child's mouth. He couldn't understand a word of what was being said, and in a moment, it was over, and she hung up the phone.

"*¿Qué quería?*" he asked.

"What did he want? Nothing. It was a wrong number. He thought we were a bookstore. He was calling from Nebraska."

"From where?"

"Nebraska. The West. Cowboys and Indians."

"The Alamo?"

"Close enough."

Collazo began to root around in the lap drawer of his desk.

"What are you looking for?" Rosa asked after a moment or two.

"I think I had a map of the U.S. I want to see this place."

Rosa grew restless with his search. "What do you want to see Nebraska for?" she asked.

"Oh, Cristina wants me to retire; says I'm too old to be a deputy. She said she wants to go traveling. I'm willing to go somewhere, but I can't think of where to go. Have you ever been to Nebraska?"

"Nobody's ever been to Nebraska," Rosa answered. "When do we get to go on patrol?" she asked.

Collazo was taken aback by the question. He looked at his watch.

"It's one-ten in the morning. Where are we going to patrol?"

"Crimes happen at night, too," she answered, and with that she got out of her chair and strapped on her gun belt. She was going to take a turn around the city whether Collazo escorted her or not.

Almodovar walked to the door and opened it.

"I'll wait for you outside."

Collazo threw his hands up.

"Papa Dios," he prayed as he strapped on his

gunbelt. "Now you have put two women into my life. One I can handle. Two cannot be satisfied. One wants me to quit and stay out of danger. The other won't be happy until I find her a shootout."

The night air in Angustias can be cold. While it is a town on the tropical island of Puerto Rico, it is also set high in the central mountain chain. The almost constant breezes that keep the summers there temperate produce a definite chill in the fall and winter.

"It's cold out," Collazo stated to his young partner. His hope was that Deputy Almodovar would take his hint and decide to stay in the station house.

"Then we should walk quickly to warm up," she said, and started off towards the town plaza.

Collazo was nearly six feet tall, and Almodovar was barely five feet in height. This difference allowed Collazo to keep pace without much strain.

A quick view of the plaza was enough to ensure there was no activity there. After only a minute of walking, Officer Almodovar decided to head off on one of the side streets leading away from the center of town. Another side street and another were enough to convince Collazo that even if Angustias had an indigenous criminal element (which he doubted) they had decided to leave their prowling for a more reasonable hour.

The walk was no less boring to him than sitting in the station house.

"So," he said. "Tell me about yourself."

"What do you want to know?" Rosa answered, but she wasn't really paying attention to him. She was intent on every door and window they passed.

"When did you become a police officer?"

"Five years ago . . ." She stopped in her tracks, listening to the faint sounds of the night air.

"What's that?" she asked.

Collazo listened a moment. "What's what?" he answered.

"Don't you hear a squeaking sound? I think it's coming from that house." She pointed to a house across the street from them.

"That's the Rodriguez home. They got married last Saturday. It sounds like their bed is making a lot of noise. If you want, we can knock on the door and investigate. . . ."

Officer Almodovar was already walking off towards another side street.

"Where else have you worked?" Collazo asked a minute later.

"I started in New York. I walked a beat in the Bronx for a couple of years. I moved to Puerto Rico three years ago and started working for the San Juan police. Now I'm here."

29

They walked on a bit further in silence, until Almodovar was satisfied that nothing really was happening in town. She stopped on a street corner and surveyed the nearby houses.

"Does anything ever happen in this town? Do you guys ever earn your pay?"

"Which guys?" Collazo asked.

"You guys. The cops in this town."

"Aren't you one of us?"

"You know what I mean. The veterans. Have you guys ever done anything? Solved a murder? A bank robbery? Something?"

"Yup. Seven murders since Gonzalo started in sixty-four, six solved. Domestic violence. Car thefts. A shootout at Colmado Ruiz. A suicide in the prison cell. Drunken brawls. Auto wrecks. We get a lot of business. But this is not New York; it doesn't all happen on the same day. Tomorrow night will be busy for us, Friday nights always are. A lot of teenagers to keep an eye on, fights to break up, people to drive home. Yup. We earn our pay."

Rosa rolled her eyes.

"Can't wait," she said.

"*Mi'ja*, don't talk like that. You don't know what you're asking for. When the police are busy, no one is happy—people get hurt and die."

"I know. I know all of this. I just need to do something soon or I'll go out of my mind."

"Didn't we arrest two drunks yesterday?" Collazo countered.

"They passed out on the precinct doorstep. You brought them in to keep them warm. I don't really call that an arrest."

Collazo paused in thought a moment and shook with the cold of the night air.

"Well," he said, "there are two different things we can do—usually, I prefer to do one and not the other at this hour, but I'll let you decide."

"What are they?" Rosa asked, with the first spark of interest she had shown the entire week.

"Well, what I like to do some nights when I can't fall asleep in the station house is go through the unsolved cases. I figure, even if we can never put the criminal away, the practice makes my mind a little sharper."

"Any good cases?" Rosa asked.

"A few robberies—one of them was a pig, though, and I think it was chopped up and sold. Also, the murder I mentioned earlier . . ."

"Tell me about it," Rosa said.

The deputies walked back towards the station house.

"Well, it was Gonzalo's first big case, right out of college. A three-year-old girl was missing. The entire town went out to look for her and Gonzalo found her."

"Dead?"

"Dying. She died within the hour after being found. There was almost no physical evidence and, of course, no one saw anything."

"What'd she die of?"

"She bled to death. Rape and sodomy. Everyone went to the clinic to see if she would live. As sheriff, Gonzalo was in the examining room until the moment she died. He held her in his arms until her mother came. He looked into her eyes. He cried that day—he tried to resign. Ask anyone in town; they all know. Then he got angry and spent the rest of the year trying to solve the case." He pulled the precinct door open. "After you.

"He has vowed to catch the man who did it, and he studies the case file at least once a week. In 1971, he eliminated every citizen of Angustias as suspects. If the criminal still lives, Gonzalo will catch him. Do you know what he told me last week? He said, 'Criminals always return to where they've been successful.' He's still waiting for the animal to return. He's waiting for revenge, and I don't know who to pity more. . . ."

"Do you think he'd kill the guy?"

"Yup. But I wish he wouldn't. Revenge is pointless. It's like the candy the kids eat at the *fiestas patronales*—it tastes sweet at first, but it dissolves as you eat it and leaves you empty."

Officer Almodovar thought for a moment, then

went to the file cabinet and pulled out the case file. She sat at the desk and began leafing through the pages of notes and testimony. Ten minutes later she looked up to ask Collazo what was the second activity he did to entertain himself during the dark hours of the night, but he was snoring lightly, and she didn't need further clarification.

Chapter Three

The call came at just a little past one in the morning, just as Gonzalo was drifting into a deep and comforting sleep. As he hurried, squinting, to the kitchen to pick up the receiver before his wife awoke, he wondered why he still bothered. In more than twenty years of marriage, Mari had not once been disturbed by late-night callers. She had the uncanny ability to roll over again in bed and fall into an even more profound sleep than before the phone rang. This time she didn't even raise her head from her pillow. Gonzalo envied her her peace.

"Who is it?" he whispered into the phone a bit more harshly than he had expected.

"Is Mari up?" was the reply.

"Mari? It's one in the morning. Who are you?"

Gonzalo asked. His voice this time had the right harshness to it.

"It's me, Viña. Your sister-in-law. You know I wouldn't call you at this hour without a reason. Papi's in the hospital. Mari needs to come over."

The news sent a shock through Gonzalo that made him open his eyes wide and take a seat. Mari's father was ninety, but he was one of those people who seem never to diminish in physical strength or mental acuity. He still farmed seven acres of hillside land and took care of a small menagerie of animals. Just a month or two before, he had joked with the old man about who would die first.

"What do you mean, 'In the hospital'?" Gonzalo asked, though the words were pretty clear.

"He got into a fight . . ."

Viña said more after this, but Gonzalo took the receiver away from his ear for a moment and shook his head. Men of ninety don't get into fights, they get attacked. Gonzalo asked his sister-in-law to start the story from the top, omitting no detail, and this is the essence of what she reported.

"Papi and Mami went to bed, Mami says around ten o'clock, just when the news was starting. A little while later, maybe eleven, Mami heard something that woke her up. She woke up

Papi. Mami says he ignored her, but then the dog started barking. *El viejo mío* decided to get up and take a look around the house, and he got a machete from the kitchen. He rolled one of the windows open to see if he could see what was making the dog bark, but the dog was at the front of the house. Papi went to open the front door, and as soon as he turned the knob, three guys pushed the door in. Papi tried to fight them with the machete but there were three of them and they were young men."

Viña said all this without pausing, and Gonzalo could think only the worst thoughts. What could one ninety-year-old man do against three young men?

"So what happened? Did they rob your parents? Did they touch your mother? What happened?" Gonzalo asked.

"What happened? Mami came out of the bedroom screaming at the three guys. They ran away. Mami called a neighbor because Papi couldn't get up off the floor. The neighbor brought him to the clinic, and the nurse on duty called me at home. We tried to treat him there, but we had to transfer him to the hospital in Aguada."

"He was that bad?" Gonzalo asked.

"Well, yes and no. He needed to be hospitalized. He is stable, though. The main problem was that the three guys also went to the clinic looking for medical help."

"He hurt them?" There was a note of pride in Gonzalo's voice. He had no sympathy for anyone who would beat an old man.

"Did he hurt them? Are you kidding me? You know how he keeps his machetes."

Gonzalo began to feel for the criminals when he thought of the razor edge Don Emiliano kept on his machetes. Even the one kept in the kitchen for such low work as opening coconuts and weeding the kitchen garden was sharp enough to cut through leather. Gonzalo had found that out the hard way when he first came to know his father-in-law, years earlier.

"What kind of damage did he do?"

"A lot. The doctors didn't let me go near them. They thought I might have a bad reaction to seeing them."

"What do you think?" Gonzalo asked. He knew Viña was no different from his wife when it came to temper. If they had a good enough reason, they could be downright vicious.

"I was under control," Viña answered.

"Okay. So what else?"

"Well, Papi's being treated now. Nothing life-threatening, but Mari should come over to see him if possible. He's going to be in the hospital for a few days. I think he's a little afraid to be here."

"Hasn't he ever been in the hospital before?"

"You kidding? Never. Mami never stayed in a hospital either. We were all born at home."

"Right, well, let your parents know we'll be over there before lunch tomorrow. For tonight, I'll let Mari get her sleep. We'll spend the weekend and take it from there, okay?"

Gonzalo sat up a few minutes trying to recreate in his mind the epic battle his father-in-law had fought. Then he turned his attention to rearranging the precinct schedule for the next few days. Finally, as he got back into bed, he thought of how he would break the news to his wife. This aspect bothered him the most and kept him up for more than an hour.

Mari woke up some minutes before Gonzalo, which was unusual. Of course, she had slept soundly through the night, while his sleep had been severely interrupted. When he opened his eyes, she was already out of the bathroom, fixing her hair into a ponytail and humming.

"Mari," he said, padding his way to the bathroom. "We have to talk."

There can be no more ominous way of beginning a conversation. Mari stopped her humming while Gonzalo closed the bathroom door.

"What's the matter?" she shouted at the bath-room door.

"It's about your father," Gonzalo shouted back.

"What about my father?" Mari asked, and Gonzalo could hear the rising tension in her voice. He hadn't started the way he had planned.

"Don't get me wrong. He's all right. He's just in the hospital."

Mari opened the bathroom door and stood there with her hands on her hips.

"What?" she demanded.

Gonzalo sought refuge by shoving a toothpaste-covered toothbrush into his mouth, but Mari made her demand again, and it was clear there would be no appeasing her short of a complete discussion of her father's situation. Gonzalo disclosed all he knew about the case.

"But he is stable now. Not in any danger."

Mari had already walked away and begun rummaging through the closet for clothes to pack. Gonzalo came out of the bathroom and headed for the kitchen.

"When did you find out about this?" Mari called out to him.

Gonzalo came back to the bedroom door.

"I got off the phone at about one thirty in the morning."

Mari looked at him as though he were an accomplice to the three men who had put her father in the hospital.

"Why didn't you wake me?"

"To tell you what? No hospital is going to let you see your father at three in the morning. He has to sleep. Don't worry. We'll be there before lunch. We'll have breakfast. We'll make a brief visit to the precinct, then we'll be on our way."

Mari accepted the terms, and Gonzalo went about the business of making breakfast. When it was done, he woke their daughter and got her ready to come to the table.

"Okay, Sonia," he told her. "You're going to have your breakfast now, then I'm going to get you ready to stay in Grandma's house for a few days, okay?"

The little girl, seven years old, readily agreed but began to have second thoughts while she ate her cereal.

"Why do I have to go to Grandma's house?" A sensible question.

"Mommy and Daddy have to go away on business," Gonzalo tried to explain, but this wasn't good enough for the little girl.

"What business?" she asked.

"Police business."

"Mommy's not a policeman," Sonia pointed out astutely.

"But I need to take her, sweetheart. She's my wife."

Sonia ate another spoonful of cereal. "I'm your daughter," she said.

Mari took over the conversation.

"Look, Sonia, me and Daddy need to go somewhere. Today is Friday. We will be back on Monday. You will stay with Grandma for a few days. That's all. Understand?"

"Yes," Sonia said, beginning to pout. "I understand, but I don't like it."

"Sweetie, I don't like it either, but we have to do it, okay?"

Getting Sonia ready for the stay at her grandmother's house was the work of only a few minutes. She was one of those self-disciplined children that every parent hopes for and tries to mold, but who comes to be the way they are because of something God did. She had stayed over at her grandmother's house, only a hundred yards down the road, many times, and always enjoyed her visits. Her grandmother, Gonzalo's widowed mother, kept plenty of animals though she had only a few hours of mobility a day due to emphysema and painfully swollen legs that resulted from poor circulation. The little girl was a boon to her grandmother because at the age of seven she could think of nothing better than to feed, water, and groom the goats, chickens, ducks, and rabbits that each had a place on her grandmother's acreage.

Sonia Gonzalo the senior, for whom Gonzalo's daughter was named, is someone who should be introduced properly. Gonzalo's mother was twenty when he was born, but he wasn't her first child. Married at the age of seventeen, Sonia had given birth twice before Gonzalo came along. Both children had died within a month. This was not uncommon for rural Puerto Rico in the early forties. Two other children born after Gonzalo also died within a month or two of birth; then his little sister Rosalinda was born.

Rosalinda was still living, but she may as well have been dead. She left home for New York at the age of fifteen, and since then had blown about the United States like the human-sized tumbleweed she had once sent a picture of. She called herself a journalist, but she spent at least as much time working in factories and in diners or not working at all. In more than twenty years, Rosalinda had managed to write six times and call six times and visit exactly once. The visit was arranged and paid for by Gonzalo, the calls were always collect, and the letters never had a reliable return address. More than emphysema and swollen legs, Sonia suffered from a broken heart and fits of sighing.

Gonzalo's daughters—he had two others who were grown and moved away—were the only solace for Sonia Gonzalo. That, and cigarettes, a habit she had picked up once she was widowed some twenty years earlier. Even Gonzalo, a model son in his care and visits, could not bring a smile to his mother's face the way even a photo of the younger Sonia could. Dropping the little girl off at any time of day or night was never a problem and needed no elaborate explanations. That suited Gonzalo on this particular morning.

The station house was a different question. While he had often left Angustias in the care of Emilio Collazo and Hector Pareda, he had never left new officers in their care. More importantly, this was a Friday and Friday nights were special in Angustias as in much of the Western world. *Viernes Social* was a time for young people to get together at friends' houses and drink. The main objective was to find someone to spend the night with, perhaps even the entire weekend. While liquor helped in this objective, it also led to fist-fights, erratic driving, and general rowdiness. Without an effective police presence, even the sleepy little town of Angustias could get out of control.

Arriving at the station house, he was somewhat surprised to see four of his deputies hunched over one of the computers, reconnected and set up in the corner furthest from the construction work, which had already begun for the day.

"What are you guys doing?"

"Shhh. Iris is trying to hook us up to the files in San Juan," Hector said.

"What files?" Gonzalo whispered.

"Of the criminals. Fingerprints, case files, everything. This little machine is amazing," Collazo spoke now.

"She looked up some of my cases in New York. They had everything, and through San Juan, we have access. Even my picture's in there. Each case only takes about nine or ten minutes to load once you make the connection," Officer Almodovar added.

"Isn't it faster to just call if you need something specific?" Gonzalo asked.

"Sure, but if you don't know exactly what you want, you can just take a look around. You can take your time. No clerk in New York is going to let you do that. I'm telling you, Chief, one day computers are going to play a huge role in law enforcement—mark my words."

Rosa gave him a knowing grin. Gonzalo wondered whether he should take the time to ask what project she had in mind, but he remembered his wife sitting in the car and his promise to her that his business would only take five minutes. He pulled Collazo and Hector aside and explained why he was taking off on such short notice.

"Get ahold of Officer Fernandez, put him on a split schedule. Give either Rosa or Iris a late schedule. I want *Viernes Social* to be smooth to-night. Everyone has to know there will be no fool-ishness just because I'm gone a few days. Understand?"

"Son," Collazo spoke. "You think too much of yourself. People aren't waiting for you to leave to become bad. Go be with your family. Angustias won't fall apart over the weekend just because you're in Rincón."

Gonzalo turned toward the door unconvinced by the old man's words. He turned to his deputies again.

"Make sure these construction workers don't waste the whole day with coffee breaks. I want to see some progress when I come back," he said, not able to think of another admonishment.

"Don't worry, boss," Hector said. "My cattle prod's in my locker."

With that the deputies returned to the wonders on the computer screen, and Gonzalo walked out to his car.

Chapter Four

The drive from Angustias to Rincón is long. The most direct route is over a series of panoramic highways designed by the state government to increase tourism through the center of the island. The views from any part of this stretch of blacktop can be awe-inspiring, and this presents its own particular set of problems. There are few actual attractions aside from the view in the area and fewer signs indicating where rest stops and gas stations are. Island natives rarely stop to take in the vista, preferring to drive through to their destination as quickly as possible—in much the same way that New York residents don't look up at skyscrapers. Tourists, however, will occasionally come to a stop in the middle of the road (there often is no shoulder) to take pictures or study maps. Gonzalo had been called out to accidents caused in this way several times. This morning, the roads were pretty much clear. He and Mari were on them by seven-thirty.

In the whole time they were in the car (a little more than two hours) there was only one topic of discussion.

"Did she say anything about his condition?" Mari asked.

She had asked the exact same question several times before getting into the car, and Gonzalo was beginning to be sorry he had not woken his wife at one in the morning to handle the call herself.

"Well? Did she say anything about his condition? Anything at all?" she insisted.

"Like I told you five times already, she said he was in the hospital. It didn't sound life-threatening to me, but he's an old man, more than ninety. I'm sure they wanted to keep him for observation even if his problems were minor. I'm also sure your sister would have said something if it were serious—"

"Why didn't you ask her? Why didn't you get more information? What's the matter with you, can't you ask questions? Can't you speak up?"

Gonzalo spent the rest of the trip thinking any number of logical reasons why he did not have all the information Mari wanted. He held all these back, biting his tongue, knowing that Mari's problem was her nervousness and that his excuses would do nothing but make matters worse. For the remainder of the ride, Gonzalo simply raised a finger whenever Mari seemed ready to go on the offensive again. He put a little more pressure on the gas pedal, and they arrived in Rincón in less time than usual.

The town of Rincón has been an independent municipality for over two hundred and fifty years. The word Rincón means corner and aptly describes the town's appearance on the map. Located between the slightly larger cities of Aguada and Añasco, the bulk of Rincón juts out into the Caribbean Sea. The beaches are still pristine, and there are annual surfing competitions. The turn-of-the-century lighthouse warns everyone that there is no safe anchorage in that area.

Like most of the smaller towns in Puerto Rico, the majority of citizens do not live near the center of the city. Instead, the city center holds the government offices and the Roman Catholic church along with a good number of small businesses—a bank, two grocery stores, a pizza parlor with three video arcade machines, and a plaza that was once quaint and appealing but which was ruined in the eighties in an effort to modernize its appearance—a gazebo and several trees were removed and a small band shell that has rarely been used was put in its place.

Mari's sister lived in one of the neighborhoods

on the fringes of the town itself. Barrio Calvache is distinguished from the surrounding country-side by Route 115, which runs through it for a mile or so. Along this road, Mari's brother keeps a small grocery store for those who would rather not make the trip into town, and on this road there is a gas station and a *panadería* where people buy their bread and newspapers each morning. Not more than a hundred yards off this road, Virginia Ayala has her home, her husband, and her three sons. By the time Gonzalo drove into the driveway, Virginia (Viña, as her friends call her) was visiting with her father. The teenaged sons were the only ones home at that hour, and they came out onto the porch when they heard the car pull up. Mari jumped out of the car and began her interrogation of the boys.

"How is your grandfather?" she asked.

"*¿Abuelo? Abuelo está como coco.*" Roughly translated, "Grandpa's as tough as a coconut." This news from the youngest son, a boy then of only fourteen years.

The oldest son added, "Your old man's a hood-lum. He chopped up some Dominicans. You should ask if they survived."

"*Dime todo,*" Mari demanded. "Tell me every-thing."

In their hurried and confused way, the three boys were able to say a great many words without

49

adding anything to the story as Viña had told it to Gonzalo or Gonzalo had told it to Mari the first time. For some reason, however, Mari seemed much more satisfied by this third-hand telling of the story.

"Is that everything?" Mari asked at the end of the story.

The boys tilted their heads trying to satisfy her desire for detail, but there was nothing else for them to add. "If you're worried, go see him," the middle one said.

"But when are visiting hours?" Mari asked.

"I don't know. Doesn't Luis have a badge?" the boy answered.

These words were fateful, and Gonzalo winced when he heard them. While most of the world is ready to believe that a police badge is an automatic pass through every closed door, Gonzalo knew that relying on the authority of the badge to scare people into giving him access where he would otherwise be forbidden was problematic at best. If the doctor decided to call his bluff, Gonzalo could wind up sitting in a waiting room until the doctor conveniently remembered him hours later. If it were actually police business, Gonzalo might be tempted to pull out his handcuffs and use them. That course of action was not an option in this case.

"That's right. You can get us in. Come on,"

Mari said, and she was out the door before Gonzalo could mount a defense.

By the time Gonzalo got outside, Mari was strapped into her passenger-side seat, watching him through the window, wondering why he was so slow. There would be no point in arguing, so Gonzalo climbed into the car and drove off toward the hospital.

Things at the hospital began just as he feared. They went to the reception desk and were told that visiting hours would not start until one in the afternoon. Mari explained she was the daughter of the patient, and the receptionist said she would have to speak to a supervisor.

"Wait, wait, wait!" Mari said. "Forget your supervisor. My husband is a police officer. Show her your badge, Luis."

What could Luis do but roll his eyes and bring out his badge? Luckily for both Mari and him, the receptionist was new to her job and not yet jaded or cynical of Gonzalo's authority. She gave them a visitor's pass and let them go on through.

"Don't do that again," Gonzalo whispered as they walked the halls.

"Do what?" Mari asked.

"Tell people I'm a police officer."

"Why not?" Mari resisted.

"Because."

"Because why?"

What answer could he give his wife at this point? Could he tell her that some people didn't like cops? Or that he didn't enjoy forcing people to do things for him just because he had a badge? As they approached his father-in-law's room, he decided to state a reason his practical-minded wife could readily sink her teeth into.

"Now that the receptionist knows I'm a cop, if any emergency occurs, she can ask me to take care of it and I have to do it. When I show my shield, I assume legal responsibilities."

"But you're on vacation," Mari said, pushing open the door to her father's room.

In fairness to Mari Gonzalo, in the more than twenty years since they'd been married, she had not once until that time asked her husband to flex his authority in such a way. She would not have done so on this occasion, except that she felt desperate to be at her father's side.

Inside the room the old man was reclined at an angle halfway between lying and sitting. Mari's mother was at one side of his bed and Viña was on the other. The room was shared by a second patient, who was hidden by a curtain drawn most of the way.

"*¿Cómo estás, Papi?*" was the first thing Mari asked. "How are you doing?"

"*¿Qué? ¿Ya no pides bendición ni dices hola?*" was

the old man's reply. "Don't you ask a blessing or say hello anymore?"

His response was a clear sign that there was no need to worry about his health. There was a four-inch-square bandage taped to the bald area at the top of his head, and his right wrist was in a kind of splint. There was dark bruising under his left eye.

"Are you hurt?" Mari asked.

"They broke a few ribs, *negrita*, but I'll live," the old man answered.

The use of her childhood nickname, *negrita*, made Mari want to cry and put her head on his chest and have her father run his fingers through her hair. He hadn't done that since thirty years before when she had stamped her foot on the ground and commanded him never to take the liberty again. She had felt herself too old then, and it was only now as she realized her father was nearing the end of his life that she began to calculate all she had lost through her youthful arrogance.

"They want to keep him another two nights," her mother sniffled.

Mari looked to her sister the nurse.

"It's pretty standard for a man his age. If he were fifty, they would have kept him one night. If he were twenty, they would have wrapped him up and sent him home."

Of course, Mari's father was made to tell the

entire story of what had happened the night before. His wife chimed in many details, so that by
the time Mari felt satisfied, she knew as much as
her parents did about the attack, along with information concerning the hours before and after the
event.

At the end of the story, Gonzalo had one question. "So what did the police have to say about all
this? Is there going to be a trial, or do they want
to just deport these guys?"

"I don't know. The police just asked me a lot of
questions. They didn't give me any information."

"Well, judging by the injuries you received and
the ones they got, I would guess they would want
to prosecute, but I hope not."

The women in the room protested Gonzalo's
statement. They wanted to see the attackers get all
that was coming to them, perhaps even a little
more. Mari was no less vocal than her sister or
her mother.

"How could you say that? You're a cop and you
want these guys to get off free? What if they had
killed *mi viejito?*"

"Well, that would be a different case altogether
of course, but as it turns out, your father's alive
and in pretty good shape. To prosecute these
guys means your parents would have to testify
against them in court, maybe a few times."

"So?"

"Then in the end these guys might get a couple of years in jail and after that, deportation. If I didn't know your father, if he were a victim in Angustias, and I were the one handling the case, I would tell him to press charges for the good of all mankind. But I know Don Emiliano. I like him. As a friend, I say he should consider leaving everything alone."

"That's your advice?" Mari asked, with contempt drenching her voice.

"Don't worry. It really won't be up to him anyway."

"I can't believe it. You're talking like a woman."

"Like a woman?" Gonzalo repeated. "The women in the room want to kill these guys."

"Gonzalo's right," Don Emiliano spoke up. "One of the men had his right arm removed. Another one had a few very deep cuts in his gut. The one who grabbed the machete might never use his fingers again, the doctor said. That's enough, no?"

Don Emiliano looked at his daughters and then at his wife. She turned her face away.

"After ninety years, I have done serious harm to men I don't even know. I chopped an arm off. Now you want me to say these men should go to jail? I say they've already suffered. I say they will continue to suffer without any more help from me. Send them home. If I get a chance, that's what I'll say. I'll tell any policeman, any judge, the governor, President Reagan himself. Send those boys home."

The old man tried to turn onto his side, but his ribs would not allow for that, so he turned his face into his pillow. It was clear that the talk of trials and retribution wore on him more than any pain he might have been feeling, and everyone but his wife decided it was time to end the visit. She could not think of any other place to be when her husband was hurt than at his side, so she sat stroking his hand.

Outside the room, Mari paced a moment before coming out with her take on the preceding interview.

"He doesn't know what he's doing," she explained to her husband. "People like that can't just be let go. They can't just give those guys a ticket and send them back to the Dominican Republic. They'll be on the next boat back over here. Papi has to press charges; it's the right thing to do."

Mari looked to her husband and waited for him to speak. The expression on her face told him that she expected him to see the logic in her argument. Of course he saw it; he had used the very same argument many times before.

Those not in police work would be astounded how few victims wanted to press charges against their attackers. Fear is an obvious factor: a person who has just had his or her nose broken will often not want to encounter the assailant again. More common, however, is the intense desire to have done with the matter. After all, how many people enjoy reliving the most terrifying moments of their lives the number of times required in a criminal case in front of a roomful of strangers? It was part of Gonzalo's job to convince people to put aside their fear and discomfort for the greater good of the general population. Still, he was always aware that he was asking a lot from the victims, and he did not have the heart to ask this much from his father-in-law.

"Mari," he started, "do you really think your father has lived a life this long only to have his own daughter, his youngest daughter, tell him what he should do with his life? He almost cried in there. He feels bad about what he did."

"But he did a good thing. He defended Mami. He fought off three young men."

"I know. To you, he's a hero. To me, he's a hero. Except for the three guys he fought off, you won't find anybody on the whole island who won't say your dad is a hero. But he doesn't feel like a hero. He feels like he almost killed someone."

"That's ridiculous."

"Sure. But then you've never actually killed anyone, have you? Believe me, I know. Everyone pats you on the back, but when you replay the incident in your mind, and you *do* replay it a thousand times, all you can think of is how things could have been different..." Gonzalo turned away from his wife here, and she knew tears were welling in his eyes. "Since the shootout at Colmado Ruiz, I have not gone to sleep one night without thinking of what I did then. Most times I accept it. Sometimes I wish I...I...Sometimes I think bad thoughts. You see, Mari? That's from a shootout where I won; I saved an innocent man's life. The police department gave me a medal, the governor shook my hand, the president of the United States sent me a letter wishing there were more cops like me." Gonzalo turned back to his wife, but she lowered her head to avoid seeing the tears that ran from both eyes.

"Leave your father to do whatever he wants. He's old, and last night will be with him until he's lowered into the grave."

That night, when Mari and Viña met with the other three siblings in the family, Mari convinced them all that their father should be left to decide what he wanted to do in pressing charges. While her brothers and sisters thought she was wrong in this, they had all learned when young that going against their little sister rarely worked to their advantage.

As it turned out, the case was one of federal interest and the federal government was in no rush to tell anyone what they were planning besides the detention of the assailants. When Mari and Luis, Viña and her husband got together that night at Viña's house, the possible moves of the federal prosecutors and the Immigration and Naturalization Service were the subjects of discussion until midnight, when all turned in to their quarters to end their too-long day.

Only a little later that night, and a few miles from shore, the pilot of a small boat from the Dominican Republic was finding that there was no more gasoline, though the fuel gauge still read full. Although the ship had made very good time and ridden the waves strongly, it was riding low with more passengers than it should have had, and it was taking on water at a pace that frightened the human cargo. The lighthouse of Rincón was within sight and a small craft was rapidly making its way nearer. The captain felt certain this was his employer coming out to meet his ship, but this brought him no comfort. Instead, he went into the toolbox and picked out a claw hammer and a small wrench and gripped one in each hand so firmly that his knuckles ached.

Chapter Five

Gonzalo's day had been a long one, and his sleep the night before had been disturbed, so when he put his head on the pillow this night it took less than the normal hour for him to fall asleep. Even more unusual was the fact that he did not hear the phone when it rang at a little before two in the morning. What finally woke him was the sound of his sister-in-law bustling about the house trying to get dressed and find her car keys.

He still wasn't fully awake until she quietly opened the door to the room he and Mari were borrowing from the eldest son. She tiptoed into the room and carefully chose a set of keys from a glass bowl sitting on the bureau. As she turned to leave the room, Gonzalo spoke.

"What's the emergency?" he asked in a whisper.

Viña gave a little hop from fright and dropped the keys.

"*¡Ave Maria, qué susto!*" she hissed.

"Sorry. I was whispering to keep from scaring you," he said in a normal tone.

"What about Mari?"

"You know her. Only an act of God could wake her at this hour. Anyway, what's the emergency?"

"Another boat wreck. Bodies are washing up on the beach. I probably won't be back tonight."

"I'll go with you," Gonzalo said, rolling out of bed and out from under the mosquito netting.

"What about Mari?" Viña asked.

Gonzalo looked to his wife. "I don't think she would want to go."

"I mean if you want to go that's fine, but you should leave her a note or something."

"Oh, right. In case this takes a while."

Viña laughed and left the room and Gonzalo dressed and put a note on his pillow.

"Dear Mari," it said. "Viña and I went to the beach to find dead people. Be back soon."

Viña had stacked a half dozen old blankets and a two-gallon, red plastic bottle of water onto the back seat of her car beside a large canvas first-aid kit. Gonzalo decided to take his own car. He figured he might be needed to run errands or drive people to the hospital.

Rincón is blessed with several beaches, each with a different point of beauty. *El Balneario*, the public beach of choice in Rincón, has a broad strip of sand and a sea that calmly laps onto shore as though asking permission with each wave. However, *Las Puntas*, only a thousand yards away, has waves to challenge expert surfers, and rocks that line portions of the shore and jut out to sea and eat small crafts and the unfortunates inside them.

A wave, vicious in intent and execution, had lifted a small wooden ship from the Dominican Republic several feet and pushed it onto these rocks a mile from shore. Weeks later, when the wreck was examined through underwater photography, it was found that the ship had suffered only one tear in its side, but this was large enough to drive a car through. The boat had fallen off the rock with the next wave and sank almost immediately to a shelf sixty feet below the bustle of the waves. The initial crash had tossed several passengers out of the hold and onto jagged stone and angry water. Most of the others were strewn about the ocean as the ship descended. Of these, some were able to swim away from the fateful rocks, but most were caught in the power of a small eddy that swirled them into the rocks over and again with each wave until a wave with enough force pushed them—or what was left of them—toward the beach. It was found later that two passengers never made it out of the hold and drowned with the ship.

The first sign that there was trouble was noticed by a pair of lovers on the beach at Las Puntas. After a long, laughing chase on the sand, the young man was about to begin whispering some words of endearment before moving to release bikini strings when, in the quiet, the young lady thought she heard more than the hard breathing of her lover. In fact, it was a clear cry for help. They both scanned the surface of the water and the young lady found what she thought was a hand waving to her from the white foam of the sea. It disappeared into the water.

The young man, strong and full of energy that could no longer be spent in any other way, ran to the water. Kicking off his sneakers, he dove into a wave, stroking hard for where the hand had been.

There is no truth to the notion that when a person sinks below the surface of the sea for a third time, it is generally the last time. Madeline Abreu had bobbed in and out of the water dozens of times since breaking free of the water around the rocks that sank her ship. She had been known as a very good swimmer in her hometown, but her experience had been gained in a calm lake and a lazy river. Also, she had not yet realized that a price had been exacted from her in consideration for being allowed to leave the rock that had torn at her with a stone's mercy: her left arm had been removed at a little below the shoulder, leaving a jagged flap of flesh to cover a few inches of broken bone. Her left foot had also been lacerated and smashed. There were wounds all over her body, so that when the young man finally fished her from below the sea surface, he found it difficult to get a hold on her. Everywhere she was slippery with her own blood, and the young man was afraid at first to handle her by areas that had wounds. It took only a moment for him to overcome his squeamishness.

When they finally reached shore, the young lady had already called for help, and the call had reached Viña at her home. In the minute before Gonzalo and Viña arrived, another body made it to shore. This was an older man, perhaps fifty and very heavy. He was dead, with a vicious gash running from his right shoulder down to his right knee. His right hand was split open to his wrist between middle and ring fingers. The young lady had helped the waves to put him on the beach, but was terrified by his wounds, and would not help her boyfriend with the woman he brought to shore.

As Viña arrived at Las Puntas, a third body washed onto the beach. This was a little boy, perhaps eight years of age, with a leg torn off somewhat below the knee. The main injury and cause of death was a blow to the back of his head that had caved in a portion of his skull. Gonzalo took the boy's pulse and yelled the result to Viña as she cared for the surviving victim.

Madeline Abreu was unconscious, her pulse weak and irregular. Viña looked to the young man who had pulled her from the sea.

"Do you drive? Is your car here?" she asked.

The man nodded.

"Let's go," Viña said.

The young man carried Madeline to his car with Viña following close behind.

"I'll be back!" she yelled to Gonzalo. "I'll send help."

For two or three minutes after Viña left, nothing happened. While scanning the waves for bodies, Gonzalo tried to calm the young lady, who was sitting, sobbing on a dune.

"Look," he said. "This will all be over in a few minutes. You and your boyfriend have saved a life. As soon as he gets back, you can . . ."

At that point, Gonzalo saw what looked like another body struggling in the water not more than a hundred feet from shore. He kicked off his shoes and ran for the waterline. In the water, Gonzalo wondered how long it had been since he had last swum. At least a year, he decided as his shoulders began to feel the unaccustomed strain.

At the spot where he had seen the body, there was nothing. Gonzalo dove several times, hoping to feel something or see something, but this gained nothing. He bobbed up to the surface and slowly looked around, only to find that the body he had seen was halfway to shore. He started in after it.

The woman, perhaps sixty years of age, washed onto the beach at about the same time that Gonzalo did. As soon as Gonzalo had determined that she was in fact dead, the young lady spotted another body in the water, then another was spotted before Gonzalo could get to swimming depth. He decided to go for the closest body. This body had only half a head, so he left it to wash ashore naturally and swam to the location of the other victim. He found a young girl, perhaps twelve years of age and still alive.

Gonzalo wrapped an arm around the girl and swam to shore. Near the beach he put his feet down and carried her with both arms. He put her down on the sand out of the reach of the waves and held her head on his lap while he searched her for injury. Both her knees were skinned to the bone, and the calf of one leg was shredded so that she bled profusely and in spurts.

Gonzalo looked into the girl's eyes and she

looked into his, raising a hand to his face, touching his cheek.

"*¿Cómo te llamas?*" he asked. "What's your name?"

The girl shook her head as if to refuse telling him.

"Tell me, sweetie. I won't bite you."

The girl shook her head again and her brow furled in apparent pain, and she coughed blood into Gonzalo's face again and again. At last, she breathed in a last time and looked into Gonzalo's eyes and reached for his face again. With his free hand he held her hand to his cheek, but there was no longer any force in her arm and the light of life had gone out of her eyes.

"Mister," said the young lady from behind him, "there's another body."

But Gonzalo had no ear for others. The girl in front of him took his attention and he placed his hand on her chest to begin CPR. The ribs of the girl's chest had been crushed, however, and he knew there was nothing he could do. He rose and took a step back and turned to the sea again.

By the time Viña returned, Gonzalo was exhausted and had lined more than a dozen bodies on the beach. Viña brought along two nurses, and the news that the police would be arriving soon. Bodybags were going to come with two ambulances that were en route from Mayagüez. The beach should be clean by dawn, she said. Gonzalo looked at his watch, which was not made for swimming, and found that time had stopped. He wondered when his own batteries would wind down. This was his second night in a row without adequate rest, and he was no longer young.

Another pair of victims washed up a bit further along the coastline, and Gonzalo ran to tend to them.

The first one he reached was a boy, perhaps in his early teens. More importantly, he was alive. His eyes were swollen shut, and his nose was definitely broken. He also had a ten-inch piece of wood embedded in his left thigh, but his breathing was steady. Viña and one of the nurses rushed over and began working on the boy. Gonzalo moved on to the next body.

The other victim was a middle-aged man, clearly dead, with two fingers missing from each hand with the palms torn to shreds. Gonzalo imagined the man clinging to the rocks until a wave ripped him away.

By this time, the scene at the beach had attracted several of the area residents. Two young men were helping to line up the bodies neatly along a sand ridge. They took a minute to rest after each body moved. They had taken the task upon themselves without having any idea of how draining it could be to look upon a lifeless face or witness the horrible wounds each victim had. Now that they had taken the work in hand, they couldn't back out of it.

Two other young men had decided to go out to sea on their surfboards. They attached flashlights to their hands and ran into the ocean with their boards. They whooped as the first wave came in and took them for a ride. Gonzalo couldn't believe what he saw, and stood for a moment with his mouth open wide. He wanted to yell the boys back to shore, but they were a hundred yards away and he was sure they wouldn't listen even if they could hear him above the roar of the sea. He shook his head and felt certain they too would wind up being fished out of the waves. A minute later, another body was spotted bobbing.

The two young men who had been lining up the bodies dashed to the water, apparently desperate to save a life. A minute later they had the body between the two of them and were dragging it to a resting place on the sand ridge. Gonzalo jogged up to them. The young men were not trained to find a weak pulse or other vital signs.

"What do you have here?" Gonzalo asked, kneeling beside the men and the body. He took the man's wrist.

"He's dead," one of the men replied.

"Are you sure?" Gonzalo asked, moving his hand to the man's neck.

"Feel his head, man," one of the young men said.

Gonzalo did as he was told and was inwardly revolted to feel that under the skin the skull bone moved freely. He pulled his hand away, but one of the young men insisted.

"Feel the back of his head."

At the back of the victim's head there was a hole, about two inches in diameter, which Gonzalo's fingers found immediately. When he yanked his hand away, Gonzalo cut his fingers on something sharp. He moved closer to take a look at what it was, while the two young men ran again to the sea to rescue another floating form.

Gonzalo could not believe what he saw at the back of the victim's head and so he took a closer look, nearly lying on his side to get a better angle. When he sat up again, he slowly shook his head and furled his brow, sorting through possibilities. At last he asked himself, "Claw hammer?" And then someone snapped his picture.

He looked up at the picture taker and was snapped again.

"What are you doing here?" he barked.

The photographer was a young lady, possibly not yet twenty, with shoulder-length dark hair and wearing a baseball cap. She had on gray sweats, the shirt having a name and a crest, though he couldn't tell from which college. She took another picture. The camera seemed expensive enough to belong to a professional, though he couldn't tell who the maker was. She took another picture.

"What are you doing here?" he asked again.

"I have a right to report all this," she said, snapping another photo.

"I didn't say no, but why don't you help first? These guys aren't going anywhere fast." Gonzalo got up, disgusted.

The young lady backed away.

"I'm not going to hurt you," he said.

"You're a cop, right?" she asked.

"Off-duty. How'd you—"

"You're not a doctor, because you let the nurses handle the living. Who else but a cop would look that closely at a crushed skull?" She seemed proud of herself.

"You want to make yourself useful? Photograph this guy's head. Close-ups. You got enough film?"

"You kidding me? I'm always ready. But what's so special about this guy?" She clicked and snapped away.

"I can't say until I see the pictures. Whatever it is, it'll be in the news in the morning anyway. I don't mind who takes the photos, as long as I get a copy, deal?"

"Sure. What's your name?"

"Luis Gonzalo, sheriff of Angustias. I'll be

spending tomorrow with Viña Ayala. She lives at—"

"I know her well enough."

"What do I call you?" Gonzalo asked.

"I'll take the Fifth for now, okay?"

"Whatever you want. Here, take a few close-ups of this." Gonzalo turned the victim's head and cleared hair away from the wound. The photographer knelt to get a good angle.

"There's seaweed," she said.

Gonzalo looked at the wound. "That's not seaweed," he said, moving it to one side.

"Oh man, don't even tell me what it is."

She took a dozen pictures more, from different angles, some with Gonzalo in them, some with nothing but the victim.

"What do you think?" she asked when she stopped to reload film from the pockets in her sweatpants.

"About what?"

"Murder, right?"

"Not sure. A lot of bodies are torn up in twenty different ways. Murder's a big word. Autopsy'll reveal something, I hope."

The blue lights of emergency vehicles flashed.

"Oh man, the cops. Look, I'll get you these photos, but I've got to get out of here. The bastard sergeant who usually responds to these things has already broken two of my cameras, and I can't afford another one right now. Check out those bruises on the face. Brass knuckles. I can make out choke marks with the lens. Murder, no doubt." She ran away.

Gonzalo moved close to the body again and made out all the marks the lens had seen.

"Shit," he said.

Someone grabbed one of his arms from behind and yanked him up. "What are you doing with this body?" he was asked.

"Nothing." He pulled out his badge. "I'm the sheriff of Angustias; just helping out."

The hand that had grabbed him belonged to a police sergeant with dark, angry eyes and dark hair. He had a five, possibly six o'clock shadow. Even with the wind blowing in from the sea, Gonzalo could smell him. The sergeant wore the blue uniform of a metropolitan police officer, those who work the big cities as opposed to the small-town sheriffs they often show contempt for. Gonzalo guessed he had driven in from Mayagüez, the nearest big city.

"Go home now. We've got this under control."

"I can help—"

"I said we could handle it."

"Okay, I'm tired anyway. But look after this body; I think he was murdered."

"Okay, whatever you say, sheriff of Angustias. Why don't you just go back to your town and take care of the cow thieves, and let us handle the emergency here, okay? Run along."

The officer gave Gonzalo a gentle shove toward the parking lot. Three officers had already started the process of numbering the dead with wrist tags. When the sergeant turned his back, Gonzalo walked over to the victim and looked at the tag. The young man with the broken skull was number twenty-one.

"I told you to get out of here!" the sergeant roared, and since he was very tired and nowhere near his jurisdiction, Gonzalo walked to Viña and told her he was going home. Then he got into his car and went.

Chapter Six

In the minutes it took to drive from Las Puntas to Viña's house, the adrenaline rush Gonzalo had been working under began to wear off and an uncontrollable nervousness made its way into his limbs. As he climbed the stairs and entered the living room, he felt lightheaded. Every time he closed his eyes, he saw a horrible wound or the eyes of a little girl dying in his arms. He wasn't a drinker under most circumstances, but he knew he wasn't going to fall asleep without something to deaden the images in his mind, so he headed straight for the kitchen cabinet where Viña's husband kept the liquor.

His hands shook as he opened the cabinet door and pulled down a bottle of Bacardi rum. He broke the seal and promised he would buy a new bottle to replace the one he was about to use. He poured an inch of rum onto two ice cubes in a glass and swished it in a circle inside the cup. He brought the glass to his lips and swallowed the liquor in one gulp. He repeated these motions twice more before deciding to fill the glass with three inches of rum and put the bottle away.

He sat on the sofa and sipped at his glass of rum for nearly an hour. His hope was to rid his mind of ugly images, but he succeeded only in intensifying them. When he was finished with the drink, his vision began to blur, and he rubbed his eyelids unsteadily with the back of his hand. He felt the urge to go to the bathroom and when he stood up, a wave of nausea overcame him and he sat again, vomiting with his head between his knees. He had swallowed several mouthfuls of seawater, and it would no longer stay down. He heaved again and again, even after his stomach was empty.

After what seemed an eternity with his head between his knees, he wobbled to the kitchen and fetched a handful of paper towels. With these he cleaned up most of the mess he had made.

He took a long, cold shower and crawled into bed next to his wife. Mari was sound asleep, and he thought of the great gift that had been given to her—to be able to rest so profoundly, while he tossed and turned and watched as the digital clock rolled minutes away to four in the morning.

After that, he saw no more of the clock until his wife shook him awake.

"What time is it?" he whispered, but Mari was already leaving the room.

A look at the clock told him it was just past ten in the morning. Gonzalo sat up in bed faster than he should have, and the weight of his throbbing head pushed him back onto his pillow. From his prone position, he reached for and slowly pulled on a pair of pants.

Viña was at the breakfast table on the veranda, sipping coffee. Gonzalo sat next to her and began peeling a grapefruit.

"Getting ready for work?" he asked.

"Work? I just came from working all night. I'm getting ready for bed. I might be the head nurse there, but I'm not the only one. They can get along without me for a day."

"What time did you get in?"

"Get in? I just got in now."

"Were there more bodies?" Gonzalo asked.

"How many did you stay for?"

"I saw twenty-one bodies and three survivors."

"That I saw," Viña countered. "There were thirty-two bodies and four survivors. The last survivor was a baby boy, maybe ten months. He washed up on the beach and crawled out of the water—not a scratch on him and as naked as God made him. There might be more bodies. When I left, the police said they were going to try to dive to check the ship, but you know how that goes."

Gonzalo had no idea how that went. The closest he had ever been to a shipwreck was turning over a rowboat in Lake Guajataca. The boat had decided to plummet to the bottom of the lake without so much as giving him a chance to turn it back the right way around. He had laughed at his folly, until his wife reminded him that the security deposit would not be returned to them. He asked Viña how such diving maneuvers usually went.

"The Metropolitan Police show up with their wetsuits and scuba gear. They wait around on the beach, assessing. Then the Coast Guard comes and takes over everything. I'm not even sure why they put on a show. The last time, the Metropolitan Police came in and said their equipment was faulty. The time before that . . ."

"How often do these crashes happen?" Gonzalo asked. In his mind the events of the previous night were a once-in-a-lifetime occurrence.

"Crashes? You mean as big as last night's?" Viña asked.

"Big, small, any kind."

"About once or twice a year. Other times they land safely. Other times they sink too far away for the tides to bring them in."

"How many people have been pulled out of the water?" Gonzalo asked.

"Dead or alive?"

"Both."

"Let me see. I've been head nurse for twelve years. These boats only really started coming about six years ago. Between dead and alive, I guess about two hundred in six years. Maybe more. Yesterday was the most I've ever seen at one time. A news truck showed up after you left. It'll be on the noon news, I'm pretty sure."

Having lived his life in the central mountains of Puerto Rico, Gonzalo had little idea that the problem Viña described was a constant concern to the people of Rincón. He knew only what he saw on television, and, as his sister-in-law explained, that was not the half of the story.

"For those same six years," she continued, "I can't tell you how many Dominicans have made it to shore. Hundreds. Maybe more than a thousand. They trespass through your property; they take the fruit off the trees. They take the clothes off your clothesline. They knock on your door and beg. I had one girl, maybe fifteen years old, she knocked on the door and asked for a job. She wanted five dollars a day and food."

Mari came in at this point, bringing Gonzalo coffee along with eggs and toast.

"Five dollars a day for what?" she asked.

"For dusting."

Viña crossed her arms and leaned back in her

chair. It was clear she thought the teenager's request had been ridiculous.

"What did you do?" Mari asked.

"I told her I knew how to dust my own house and that I worked for less."

"You sent her away with nothing?" Gonzalo asked, trying to keep accusation out of his tone.

"No, I didn't send her away empty-handed. I'm not inhuman. I gave her five dollars and a plate of food, and do you know what happened?" Viña asked. She waited long enough to make Gonzalo think he should be able to figure out what went on next.

"She sat on that tree stump you see there and three little boys came out of the bushes to share her food. I had to go back inside and heat up more leftovers. It turns out the boys were her brothers. They had nothing but the clothes on their backs. Two of the boys had no shoes."

The three sat at the table in silence for a moment. Gonzalo spoke first.

"And the three guys who attacked your father? They came over the same way?"

"Most likely some small boat, yeah. Sometimes they stow away on the large cargo ships that go to San Juan or Mayagüez."

"That's dangerous."

"Sure it's dangerous. Those crates weigh thousands of pounds sometimes. With a big wave, not even twenty men can keep them from moving. Remember that fishing ship about three years ago in Mayagüez? A guy, Cuban I think, stowed away with the fish in the hold. When they found him, he was buried under ten tons of tuna. I tell you, these people are crazy."

Mari spoke forcefully. "They're not crazy; they're desperate. They're poor, not like we were when we were kids. They really have nothing to eat, no toilets, no shoes, no clothes, no education . . ."

"Don't get angry with me, little sister; we lived on *pana* and *bacalao* for months at a time; we had a latrine Papi dug himself. I didn't wear shoes until I started going to school. None of us got on a raft."

"What do you mean, we didn't get on a raft? There are more Puerto Ricans in New York City than there are in San Juan."

"Well, let me tell you . . ."

At this point, Gonzalo left the table, leaving the sisters to their argument. He knew that once they got heated, there would be no point when he could get a word in edgewise. He went to the phone in the living room. It was nearing eleven in the morning, and he wanted to see if he could catch one of his senior deputies in the station house. Hector Pareda answered the phone.

"I was expecting Collazo would be there," Gonzalo said, instead of hello.

"I sent him home early. He's too old to work twelve hours straight."

"You told him that?"

"Sure, why not? It's true. He knows it."

"What about Rosa? She knock off early too?"

"You kidding me? She's excited for the first time this week. She got hold of a project here and she's been working on it with Iris."

"What are they doing?"

"Hell if I know. It's with the computers; I just stay out of their way. They spent yesterday working on this project. It keeps them occupied. Nothing happened yesterday at all."

"*Viernes Social* and nothing happened?" Gonzalo was incredulous.

"Nothing. Marrero got drunk at Colmado Ruiz. I took him home. That's it."

"How's the construction going?" Gonzalo winced in anticipation.

"Well, they almost finished putting up the wall yesterday. They're wrapping that part up now. Then they go to lunch. After that they're going to put up the wood forms for the ceiling. Tomorrow, a truck comes in to pour the cement, and we'll be pretty much done. Hey, how's your vacation going?"

Gonzalo didn't know where to begin. "Have you seen the news yet?" he asked.

"No, why?"

"A boat crashed last night. My sister-in-law's a nurse, so she was called to the scene on the beach, and I went with her. I spent a good part of the night pulling dead bodies out of the water."

"Are you kidding me?" Hector responded.

"I wish I were."

"How many?"

"Altogether, more than thirty. I dealt with about half."

"Man, pulling bodies out of the waves at night. That's spooky."

"It gets worse. I think one of them might have been murdered, but I'm not positive. In fact, let me go now and call the Mayagüez precinct. They took over and sent me home."

"Sure, sure. You want me to keep quiet about possible murder?"

"Definitely."

Gonzalo's next call was to the police precinct in Mayagüez. He identified himself as the sheriff of Angustias, but that bit of information didn't keep him from being put on hold several times as he asked about the boat crash of the night before. When he was threatened with being put on hold for a fourth time, he made a threat of his own.

"Look, Officer Velez. Do you know Deputy Chief Gomez?"

"No," came back the young voice tainted with fear.

"Well, I do. If you put me on hold, I'll give him a call. Where do you live?"

"Here in Mayagüez."

"How would you like to travel to Fajardo every day? What is that, three hours from your home? Now let me speak to someone in authority, or I promise you a transfer before the week is out."

To Gonzalo's surprise the threat worked, even though there was no Deputy Chief Gomez. A wait of half a minute more brought the watch commander to the phone.

"This is Lieutenant Perez. How can I help you?"

"Hello, Lieutenant. My name is Gonzalo; I'm the sheriff of Angustias. I happened to be in Rincón last night when the boat crash occurred. I assisted in fishing some of the bodies out of the water."

"I saw what happened over there on the news. Terrible."

"Yes, certainly terrible. As I was saying, I was there until some of your men took over and sent me home. I was just hoping to get a little information about—"

"Impossible."

"Huh?"

"Impossible. None of my men were in Rincón last night."

"But they were Metropolitan officers. Aren't you the closest Metropolitan precinct?"

"Ah, let me see. Nope. Aguadilla has a precinct. They're just as close. Arecibo has another. They're further away. In any event, I assure you, no one from this precinct was in Rincón last night."

For the moment, Gonzalo was satisfied with this response until he called the Aguadilla precinct and got essentially the same response. Then the Arecibo precinct denied having helped in the rescue at Las Puntas, and Gonzalo became worried that he would have to call every precinct on the island to find the information he wanted. He decided to ask Viña what she knew of the police, but she was of less help than he hoped.

"I've seen that same sergeant three or four other times at the beach on similar occasions. I have yet to find out his name. Doesn't really concern me, as long as someone takes the bodies off my hands. I'll tell you what: the bodies were taken to San Juan, I'm pretty sure. The living were taken to Mayagüez. The police escorted the ambulances in some cases; some of them might have had their names taken down by the staff at the coroner's office or the nurses in Mayagüez. If you really want to find the sergeant's name you could call up a bunch of very busy doctors and nurses and see if they'll help you."

"Maybe I'll just keep calling precincts."

"Well, tell me: Why do you want the sergeant's

name? Are you going to complain about something he did?"

"Actually, I wanted him to follow up on some things I had seen at the beach; I'm just hoping he did, that's all."

"And it has to be this one particular sergeant who does it?" Viña asked.

"You're right. I'll go directly to the source of information."

"Good. You do that. I'm going directly to bed."

Gonzalo's next call was to the coroner's office in San Juan. After only three complete explanations of who he was and how he was involved with the bodies that had been brought in the night before, he was allowed to speak with the deputy medical examiner.

"Well, I'm not sure what it is you want from us Sheriff Gonzalez—"

"Gonzalo."

"Right. Anyway, we only had the facilities for sixteen of the victims; the other sixteen were divided between Ponce and Fajardo. We started working at four-thirty in the morning. We brought in three people who were on vacation, myself included. We've determined the cause of death on only six so far. Frankly, I'm not sure why we're even bothering."

"The bodies were numbered with wrist tags on

the beach. Is there any way you could tell me which ones you have?"

"Sure. Hold on."

Gonzalo was patient while he heard the doctor scurry around through the room he was in and flip through some papers.

"Ah, I have it here. We have numbers nine through twenty-four. Does that help anything?"

"That's perfect. I was interested in the cause of death of number twenty-one."

"You're in luck. That's one that I did myself. It was very simple. Essentially she had a heart attack due to blood loss from a wound—"

"I'm sorry. Did you say she?"

"Certainly. Dark-skinned woman, approximately sixty years of age. No ID on her. No identifying—"

"The one I'm looking for was tagged number twenty-one. Young man, approximately thirty years old. Short dark hair, possibly a military cut. Muscular build."

It was clear none of this was registering with the doctor on the other end of the line, but Gonzalo continued his description.

"He had on a white shirt and light beige pants. He had a hole in the back of his head."

There was continued silence at the other end of the line.

"Does any of this ring a bell, doctor?"

"I don't know what to tell you, sheriff. No one fitting that description was brought to us. Maybe you got the number wrong on the beach? Would you like me to get phone numbers for Ponce and Fajardo for you?"

Gonzalo took the numbers to the other two medical examiner's offices, but no one at either of these sites had any information for him. The young man with the hole clawed into the back of his head had not made it to any of the coroner's facilities. He called several of the large hospitals on the island just in case the young man had been delivered to one of their morgues as overflow from the medical examiner's offices. This also was not the case. The body had disappeared, and in a second round of calls Gonzalo found that neither the hospitals nor the coroners had taken the name of any police sergeant. The name of one lieutenant had shown up twice: once in San Juan and once in Fajardo fifty miles away. This officer was stationed in San Juan, far removed from Rincón, and Gonzalo decided to give his precinct a call.

"Look, I'm getting ready to go home. What do you want to know?" was the watch commander's response when Gonzalo finally got him on the phone. "Yeah, Lieutenant Diaz responded to the incident at Las Puntas. He was there maybe at three o'clock in the morning. Sergeants? No. We didn't send any sergeants over. Hey, what's this about, anyway?"

Gonzalo explained what he had seen the night before, and the captain he was speaking to was silent for a minute.

"None of our sergeants were there, okay? No. I don't want to hear a description. Look, these damn Dominicans keep coming over to take jobs away from us. They all get what they deserve, you understand, Sheriff? They get what they deserve, except for the ones who live. Good-bye."

The captain hung up, leaving Gonzalo shocked at what he had heard. He made several other calls to the precincts in and around San Juan. While he could confirm the presence of several officers at the beach, no one had any record that a sergeant had been there, and no one would confirm that a sergeant fitting the general description Gonzalo gave even worked for their police department.

Late in the afternoon, when he was watching news reports on TV for the possibility that the sergeant was caught on tape, he received two phone calls only a few minutes apart.

"Luis Gonzalo? Sheriff of Angustias?"

"Yes," he answered cautiously, and braced himself for a threat.

"Your daughter is staying with your mother

across the street from your house." The caller paused.

"I know," Gonzalo answered.

"She's playing outside right now with a toy house made out of cardboard. She's very pretty, Luis Gonzalo." The caller hung up.

In the back of his mind, Gonzalo knew it would help no one if he became frantic, but it was hard for him to put this bit of information to use. He wanted to race to Angustias, but that would take an hour at best. He called Hector at the station house and told him to use extraordinary means to insure the safety of his mother and his daughter.

"Can I ask why you're so concerned now?" Hector asked.

"Nope. Maybe tomorrow."

"Okay. Sure thing, boss. I'm not a married man. I'll just sleep in your mom's house if you tell her to set up the couch for me."

"Consider it done. Thank you, Hector. You have no idea what this means to me."

"I guess not. You're coming home tomorrow, right?"

"Without fail."

"See you then," Hector said, with a calm and confidence that Gonzalo could have kissed him for.

Only minutes later, after speaking with his mother about the arrangements he wanted her to accept, Gonzalo received another phone call. It was the photographer from the night before.

"Look, I can't talk long. I'll bring you the pictures at the station house in Angustias. I've got everything you need. Also, be careful."

"Where are you?" Gonzalo demanded.

"Anyone could be listening. I've been on this phone too long already. Be careful. Trust no one." She hung up the phone and left Gonzalo with only a dial tone.

Chapter Seven

Gonzalo hung up the phone and thought of the photographer's advice: "Be careful. Trust no one." As if being careful and untrusting were one and the same. The advice of a very afraid young person who had seen too many movies. Being careful does not mean setting aside all the people who have earned your trust.

More important at the time was the call that came before the photographer's. The caller had hardly bothered to veil the threat against his daughter, but Gonzalo knew there was a great distance between saying something and doing it; most criminals are spineless. A call to his mother's house confirmed what he thought—the caller had not actually seen the girl playing in the yard. Sonia had been asleep for an hour when the call came in. Having Hector protect her put Gonzalo very much at ease—he thought of his young deputy as courageous and smart—but Gonzalo knew he would have to tell his wife of the phone call and nothing short of holding her daughter was going to reassure her.

Mari was out of the house with her sister, visiting her father in the hospital. There was just enough time for Gonzalo to wash himself and change into clean clothes before going to the hospital himself for the night visiting hours. As he entered the shower and began to let the water run over his body, he tried to measure how tired he was. It was incalculable. He had made more than a dozen phone calls and had been put on hold for a total of two, possibly three hours. He had asked the same questions over and again and gotten a jumble of answers and nonanswers. Waiting for callbacks was about as frustrating as being on hold. There was no part of police work that was more frustrating and draining for Gonzalo than cooperating with others. He preferred to work cases alone when possible and every once in a while he had to remind himself to hide his scorn for the intelligence of others. As the water beat on his head and neck, he began to feel drowsy and wish that he could solve all cases on his own. The phone rang to get him out of that fantasy and out of the shower.

"Leave it alone," the caller said, and hung up.

Gonzalo was sure he recognized the voice. He was sure it belonged to someone he had spoken to that day, but he was dripping wet and late leaving the house and so he gave the matter no serious thought. As he drove to the hospital he wondered only how many more people were lined up waiting to make a threatening call. More important, he wondered how he would discuss the threats against his daughter with Mari.

In the hospital, Gonzalo was shocked to find that there was no one at the reception area to greet him. He walked to his father-in-law's room without a single security check and without a pass. The thought came to his mind that if he were lying in the hospital bed that night, there might be an assortment of people who could come into his room and harass him as he lay helpless in his gown.

"*Ay, mi'jo*, I've been waiting for you all day," his father-in-law said. He waved Gonzalo close.

"I need a moment alone with my son-in-law, please," the old man said, and he waved the others in the room out. They filed out with looks of protest but no words. When they left, Gonzalo checked behind the half-drawn curtain. The patient in the next bed had been removed. The bed itself was neat.

"*¿Qué paso?*" Gonzalo asked.

The old man fidgeted with his sheets a moment before he could bring himself to speak.

"I'm scared," he said. Gonzalo had a speech ready that he used with victims of violent crimes, but his father-in-law raised his hand to keep him from talking.

"There were police in and out of here all day yesterday. They talked to me about what I had done. They said I was a hero."

"Well, you did do something many men half—"

"No, wait. Not like that. They thought it was good to kill Dominicans. They were laughing at what I did. I cried when they left. I told them I've helped Dominicans before."

This was news to Gonzalo. "How?" he asked.

"I've given them food, I've given them money, not much, but a little here and there. I've let a few work for me on the land, especially if there's coffee to pick. A few have slept in the tool shed."

"You live in the hills, in Atalaya Abajo. How often do these come to your door?" Gonzalo was shocked by Emiliano's revelations. The old man lived with his wife alone in the hills of Rincón, a thousand feet above sea level. The spot was secluded even by rural standards. It was possible that an illegal alien might stumble his or her way up there lost at night, but the old man's house wasn't on any important road. Gonzalo wondered whether the old man's kindness hadn't marked him as a useful accomplice to the immigrant smuggling trade. He had visions of smugglers handing out detailed maps to their human cargo: X marked the home of nice, old Emiliano Ayala, a man who would give the shirt off his back to any hardluck case.

"Every few weeks a Dominican knocks on my door. When they come from the beach, that road is the first small road they see. They know they can't stay on the main roads, or the police will pass by and ask them why they're wet. They go from house to house until they find someone who can give them a piece of bread. Sometimes that's all they want, a piece of bread so they can keep walking. What am I supposed to do, tell them I can't give them a piece of bread?"

"Well, yes. They're *illegal* aliens. They're breaking the law by coming here. You can't help them to break the law."

"*Mi'jo*, you know nothing." The old man moved his hand as though to wave Gonzalo away. He turned from his son-in-law for a minute then turned back to him with tears in his eyes.

"Do you know anything about what the *Americanos* call the Great Depression?" he asked.

Gonzalo had heard many stories from his parents. Though Puerto Rico was already a part of the United States at that time, there was little in the way of federal relief during the Depression in Puerto Rico. Occasionally a ship would pull into the harbor in Ponce loaded with two-pound bags of rice. Men would walk from wherever they lived to stand in line as long as it took to receive a handout they were no longer too proud for. The saddest men were always the ones who had arrived at the port with the dawn. These were clearly too late, but they couldn't turn away just because they saw a few thousand men in front of them. So they waited on line, moving up silently with the others hour after hour until someone started shouting on a megaphone in English that there was no more. Gonzalo's father had never been one of these late-risers.

"Do you know anything about that time? Do you know I had neighbors who dug up roots and boiled them? There were people who ate mud soup. Did you ever do that? We had two babies born in those days. Mari doesn't know about them. She doesn't have to know. They were born healthy, but there was nothing for them. There was nothing for any of us. They got skinny. Skinnier and skinnier until they died. You have children. Have you ever watched one cry itself to sleep with hunger? Ever watch one die from hunger? It's bad. After a while, even if you have food the baby doesn't want it. Did you ever sit there and have that happen to you? Did you ever sit thinking of how to murder a neighbor because they had children of their own and a bunch of unripe bananas growing on a tree?"

Gonzalo was, of course, silent. What could he say to any of this?

"See, *mi'jo*, I told you you know nothing. You're a smart man, but you know nothing. I have seen children, my children, starve to death. Their eyes sink in, their bones stick out, they shake with cold even if it's a hundred degrees out. I won't look at it again."

The old man was shaking and wiped tears from his eyes with one hand while the other clutched at his ribs. Gonzalo didn't know whether he was crying from physical or emotional pain, and he began to get nervous. It was more than a minute later when Emiliano was able to speak again and he did so with more force than Gonzalo had ever witnessed in him.

"I won't see another person starve in front of me. I give money to those Ethiopian children every time I see them on TV. Every time. I won't look at another person starve. Politicians can say whatever they want. The lawyers can do whatever they want. I don't say they're right; I don't say they're wrong. All I say is what I can and can't do. If those boys had asked me for food when I opened the door, I would have given them a feast.

If Dominicans come to me tomorrow, I'll give them food, work, clothes. But now I'm afraid."

The old man bit his lip to keep from crying.

Gonzalo took his hand. "What are you afraid of?" he asked.

"The police."

This was a shocker. Emiliano had just declared his defiance of the law.

"What about the police? They're not going to put you in jail for helping immigrants."

"I'm not so sure of that, but that doesn't worry me. I'm ninety years old. If they want me to go to jail, I'll go. I'm not afraid of jail."

"Then what?"

"I'm afraid of the police," Emiliano said, putting emphasis on the last word. "I'm afraid of what they might do to Cristina. She's younger than me by ten years, but she has arthritis. When I told them I've helped immigrants in the past, they said they might have to come to my house and arrest me and her. I'm afraid, Luis. What if . . . what if . . ."

"Nothing like that is going to happen. They were probably fooling around with you."

"No! They were laughing, but they meant what they said. I'm sure of it. I want to know—can they do it? Can they take us to jail? I mean both of us. Me, I don't care."

"Don Emiliano. Legally, if they wanted to

cause you trouble, they should have done it over this incident. Look. If they bother you again, say nothing, say three little words: 'I want a lawyer.' "

"That's four words."

"Whatever, just don't say more than that. I guarantee you, those words will scare any cop away from you. Arresting you would be a public-ity nightmare for them."

Gonzalo paused a moment. His speech seemed to have no calming effect on his father-in-law. The officers who had visited him had done a good job of scaring him. A thought crossed his mind, and he decided to speak it out loud.

"Was one of these officers a sergeant with dark hair and a five o'clock shadow? Maybe forty years old? A *Metropolitano?*"

"No. No. These guys were *gandules* like you. Both young, very young. Maybe not even twenty. Why?"

"No reason. I thought I might know who it was. I don't. But don't worry. If you want me to track these guys down . . ."

The old man waved him off. "Bring in the oth-ers," he said.

Gonzalo moved to the door.

"Wait. One more thing. I need someone to go into my tool shed. There are three bunches of ba-nanas hanging there. They should be ripe now. Bring them into the house—give two to Raul for his store. Eat the rest before they go bad. There. Now you can get the others."

With the entire family in the room, Don Emiliano seemed calm, almost happy. They discussed his scheduled release the next morning—who would pick him up, where he would go. It was decided he would stay in Viña's house a few days to satisfy her that he was all right. Then he could return to his own home and live his life as he had liked to live it for most of a century. The family left when the nurse made her fourth visit to the room to inform them that visiting hours were over.

At Viña's house, much of the talk centered on what Don Emiliano had discussed with Gonzalo during the mysterious conference, but aside from letting it be known that Emiliano was irrationally fearful of prosecution and that his fears had been pretty much dispelled, Gonzalo would not go into detail. By eleven that night each had gone to his or her own home except for Mari and Gonzalo, of course, and Cristina Ayala, who was staying with one of her sons until her husband was out of the hospital.

Gonzalo told Mari about the call concerning their daughter as they were both preparing for bed. He expected the revelation to lead to a fury of packing and a nighttime drive back to Angustias. She took the information better than he had hoped.

"How could you not tell me?" she hissed, not wanting to rouse anyone in the house.

"I just did tell you. When else was I supposed to do it? You weren't here when the call came. The hospital was a bad place for it. Look, Hector's there now. You know Hector; nothing gets past him. The call was a fake. The caller wasn't looking at her when he said he was. If I know my deputy, the squad car is parked right out in front and all the other deputies know about the phone call by now."

"All right, all right. Enough. We pack first thing in the morning. As soon as Papi's home, we're leaving. You understand me?"

"Don't talk to me that way, Mari. We're not on opposite sides here. That's what I had planned. We'll be in Angustias before lunch if we're lucky."

After making her husband call his mother's house to speak to Hector personally, Mari calmed down considerably and climbed under the mosquito netting and into bed. Gonzalo climbed in after her.

"I tell you," he started, "that Hector is something else. He picked up the phone before I even heard it ring. He's got reflexes I never had at his age. You were worried. He's the best . . ."

Gonzalo took a close look at his wife in the darkness of the room. Her eyes were already closed and her breathing was regular and heavy.

In the two minutes it took him to make the call and confirm his daughter's safety, she had fallen into a peaceful slumber, leaving behind the cares that had troubled her only moments earlier. She had always said that the bed was good for only two things and talking wasn't one of them.

An hour later the phone rang and Gonzalo rushed to pick it up, knowing he was the only person still staring at the ceiling in the house.

"Hello?"

"Luis Gonzalo of Angustias?"

"Who's this?"

"You think one of your deputies can stop us?"

"I don't know. Why don't you tell me what I should think," Gonzalo answered.

"Keep asking questions and both your men won't be enough," the caller said.

Gonzalo tried to think of something appropriately macho as a reply, but the caller hung up before he could come up with anything. Instead, he went back to bed, where he took more than an hour to fall asleep having been unable to think of a strategy more useful for dealing with these threats than the one already agreed upon with his wife.

On the other end of the line, the caller, a police lieutenant, entered into an interesting conversation of his own.

"I can't do it, *jefe*. It would be suicide. I'm not

kidding. We can scare this Gonzalo guy without doing anything like that."

"Look. You thought a few phone calls were going to chase him out of Rincón. Instead, he decided to stay overnight. Believe me, a man who isn't afraid when you threaten his daughter cannot be dealt with lightly. There is a lot at stake here for everyone. Now, just tell me what information you have on his deputies."

Nestor Ochao answered.

"Well, sir, I looked them up in the computer. Pretty recent files, updated a month ago. One officer, Emilio Collazo, he won't be a problem . . ."

"How did you determine that?" the caller asked.

"Well, Commander . . . not to sound too prejudiced against men of a certain age, but this Collazo is seventy-seven years old . . ."

"How old's his gun?" the commander asked.

"You're right, you're right. Still, I think the one to really worry about is the younger one, Hector Pareda."

"Why? Because he's young?"

"No, sir. If this . . . project you want to carry out turns into a shootout, Hector was tied for best scores in marksmanship—"

"At the academy?"

"No. In department history. Tied with three others. None of the others are still active. Also, if this turns into a car chase, this Pareda guy has the best obstacle and straightaway track records in the department. In fact, before joining the force, he was stopped for speeding on the *número dos*. Want to know his speed?"

"Let me guess—a hundred miles an hour."

"One hundred and forty-two."

"Jesus. What is he? Supercop?"

"No. His academy record shows he often acted before thinking. Still, if this turns into a shootout or a chase, we could be in trouble, sir."

"Good. I'm glad you identified the problem. Lieutenant, if you don't want to take this Pareda on, you know what you have to do. Don't let it turn into a shootout or a chase. Get in, get out, give this Gonzalo character something to think about. Something other than this incident on the beach. The media has already moved on. Give Gonzalo a reason to do the same."

"All right, sir. Tomorrow I'll pick the men, you get me the clearances I need and we can meet again tomorrow night. Ten?"

"That's good. Sergeant, get yourself ready. You'll be going into Angustias no later than Monday morning. Understand?"

"Yes, sir. Not a problem, sir," the sergeant answered.

Chapter Eight

That Sunday morning, Hector rolled from his side to his stomach and fell off the couch that Gonzalo's mother had provided him. It was the fourth fall onto the cold, hard ceramic tile floor he had endured that night, and though it was only a little after sunrise and he wasn't due in at work until noon, he decided to start his day. He examined his face in the bathroom mirror and found a small bruised area on the right side of his jawline and a nickel-sized welt forming high on his forehead. He wondered how he would explain the injuries if anyone asked. "I hurt myself sleeping," seemed more pathetic than the old line about running into a door, but he decided the truth was less complicated than any possible fabrication.

By the time Gonzalo's mother and daughter

stirred themselves from their sleep, Hector was dressed in street clothes and ready to be of service.

"I put coffee on. Do you want me to start on some eggs and bacon?" he asked no one in particular.

Little Sonia said "yes" with enthusiasm, but her grandmother overruled her.

"Men don't belong in the kitchen," she said with firmness.

"But Doña Sonia, I'm a bachelor. I cook every day. Eggs and bacon are—"

"If you want to make yourself useful, go out and cut down some weeds. Better yet, harvest me some bananas."

"It's six-thirty in the morning," Hector protested, but he knew his words would only make things worse.

"Six-thirty? Why, my husband, Luis Senior, may God rest his soul, used to be on the road to work eight miles away by four-thirty every morning. By six-thirty, he could have cut five bundles of sugar cane and tied them up. Why, I remember—"

"Okay, okay. My fault, Doña Sonia. If you want bananas, you will have bananas. Just let me know where there is a machete."

Gonzalo's mother pointed to one kept jammed behind the sink counter with only the handle showing. The handle had broken some years earlier, and been reinforced with copper wiring tightly wound around it so that it was precisely the most uncomfortable handle possible. Hector pulled it from its hiding place to find the blade had been honed so often in its lifetime that it had lost two inches of its original three-inch width.

"How old is this machete?" Hector asked.

Sonia was already laying out the strips of bacon. "That machete has been there since my husband died ten years ago. It was old when Luis brought it from the tool shed. Maybe twenty years?" She spoke without looking at the deputy and seemed to ask his opinion on the matter.

Banana trees are self-propagating and bear fruit once in their lifetime. The root ball of one plant will give birth to another directly adjacent before the fruit becomes ripe. The main difficulty in harvesting them is their height. The average banana tree stands some eight or nine feet high, but some can grow to double that.

The trees that faced Hector as he stepped out through Sonia Gonzalo's back door were all nearly twenty feet high. He walked a bit further into the underbrush, but every banana tree he spotted suffered from gigantism. He headed back toward the trees nearest the house and took a backhand swipe at one of them with the machete. The blade went through the papery trunk so smoothly, the tree stood unbothered a moment in much the same way a table setting sits when a master magician has pulled the table-cloth from underneath it. Then, very slowly, the top of the tree began to slide off its base because the machete had gone through at an angle. Where top and bottom met, the junction was wet with sap.

" 'Bout time," Hector said as the top of the tree with its fanlike leaves and ripening fruit slid to the ground. It sat next to its base, a half size replica of its former self, as Hector stepped to it and sliced the bunch of bananas that grew droop-ing from the tree top.

He walked the cluster of forty or so fruits to a wooden shed behind Doña Gonzalo's house and hung it from a cooper wire loop suspended from a center beam. There were three other banana clusters hanging from the beam in different stages of perfection. Hector picked a bunch that had reached its apex and brought it into the house.

Inside, the younger Sonia was already finish-ing a simple breakfast of scrambled eggs smoth-ered in ketchup. Before Hector could get his plate to the table, she had scampered off her chair and back to the room reserved for her use.

"Tell me again why you're here," Doña Sonia asked.

"I'm not sure. Gonzalo called me at the station

house. He said someone had called him at his sister-in-law's house and made some vague threat against his daughter. He said he wasn't too alarmed, but thought it would be a good idea if I kept a close watch while he was away. Sleeping on your sofa is about as close as I can get. Did he tell you anything different?"

"No. I guess he's working on some difficult case," Gonzalo's mother replied. There was some small pride in her voice. After all, while her son more often settled disputes over cattle, he did investigate the occasional homicide, and he had been commended for his work many times.

"Well, that's just what bothers me. He's not working on any case that I know of. He did say he had worked on that shipwreck the other night, but that can't be connected to this threat. Maybe it is, but I just can't see how. Anyway, he'll be back soon enough. Then we can ask all we want."

They finished their breakfast in silence, each of them a bit more worried about the sheriff of Angustias than they let the other know.

At the station house, Officer Rosa Almodovar was beginning to nod off after doing nothing at all for the last three hours. Deputy Collazo had stepped out to the church to be at least a small part of the Sunday morning services.

Almodovar awoke when she heard the sound of someone struggling at the door. She shook her head briskly and looked around her to get her bearings. When she looked at the door, there was the corner of a manila envelope making its way through the too-narrow space at the bottom. She got up quietly and yanked the door open.

"What are you doing?" she demanded of the young lady crouching at the door. The lady was wearing a black sweatsuit set and sunglasses.

"Is the sheriff in?"

"No. What are you doing?"

"I want to leave these for him. He asked for them. They are very important; please make sure he gets them as soon as he gets in."

Officer Almodovar took the envelope in hand and began to feel it, trying to guess what was inside. "Pictures?" she asked.

"Can we talk about this inside?" the photographer said. She was looking around her as though she expected snipers, and this made Deputy Almodovar take a look around as well. When she found nothing, she decided the person at the door might just be crazy.

"Sure. Come on in," Rosa answered and led the photographer inside by the elbow.

"Look. I don't want any trouble, you understand," the photographer said, taking the seat that was offered her. "I don't even want to publish these. I just want to give them to your sheriff and leave." She made a move to get out of her chair.

"Sit. Now I'm not going to bite you. Sheriff Gonzalo is a reasonable man. He's not going to do anything to you. You've given him the pictures. Are the negatives in here?" Rosa asked.

"Why do you want the negatives?" the photographer answered. It was clear she thought she had definitely given the pictures over to the wrong person.

In Officer Almodovar's mind the pictures were most likely incriminating evidence against her sheriff; perhaps photos of an adulterous tryst. Shoving the envelope under the door was most likely part of an extortion attempt. Being the only officer in the station house, she tried to cut the best possible deal.

"We need the negatives to make sure no more copies are made. It's very simple." Almodovar felt like she was teaching the extortionist how to negotiate blackmail.

"Oh my God!" the photographer exclaimed. "You want to cover this up too. Isn't there a single cop on this island who doesn't want those people forgotten?" She felt hopeless and had resigned herself to her fate.

"What are you talking about?"

"The dead. Have you no respect for all the dead?" the photographer answered.

Officer Almodovar was only further confused by this response.

"Here. Let me take a look at these," she said, and broke the seal on the envelope.

The pictures that first met her eyes were those of Gonzalo attending the murdered victim. Then close-ups of this victim, including pictures of the back of his head where it was clear through his short hair and drying blood that there was a hole the size of a half-dollar. Rosa rushed to the lap drawer of Collazo's desk and pulled out a magnifying glass she had often seen him use.

Close inspection of the wound showed that the edges had a peculiar triangular marking, something like a widow's peak. There was also a quarter-sized mark visible through the hair at the back of the skull and one at the hairline on the right temple. It seemed to Officer Almodovar that the man had been beaten with both sides of a claw hammer. The wounds were consistent with those she had seen on a child beaten to death in the Bronx the year she left New York for the safety of Puerto Rico.

Other photos were just as gruesome. There were close-ups of people missing limbs or torn open with a jagged edge. There were also a great many that had been taken from behind the branches of some bush on the beach. In these there were other officers and Gonzalo no longer appeared. Four pictures showed the disposal of the murder victim. Two officers carried him off the beach in one photo. The next showed a third officer opening the trunk of a police cruiser. The third showed the body being tucked into the trunk, only the arms still showing as they were being positioned. The last photo showed the cruiser driving away perpendicular to the camera's line of sight. With the magnifying glass, the driver's face was clear as were the sergeant's stripes on his shoulder.

Other pictures showed a lieutenant was on the scene directing the movements of his men but never touching a dead body. The last pictures in the bunch showed Viña holding a naked infant, who did not understand in all that he saw that his parents were most likely lying face up on the sand, lifeless. In one photo, the child clearly beamed with joy, not yet knowing what the words "ward of the state" would mean for him.

"Did you take these?" Rosa asked.

"Yes."

"Where?"

Of course, there was only one place on the island where the pictures could have been taken.

"Do you know who these officers are?" the photographer asked.

"Never saw them before."

"I've seen them one other time. The first time I saw a boat sink on Las Puntas. That was maybe four months ago. The same officers, the same lieutenant. The sergeant takes control for a few minutes, then he leaves and the lieutenant takes over. I think your sheriff thought there was a murder committed on the body they put in the trunk. I think so too. None of the other bodies were put in a trunk. I was there all that night. The sergeant and the other guys carrying the body never came back."

"Too bad you didn't take a picture of the license plate."

"I did. Use the magnifying glass."

Officer Almodovar did as she was asked. The license plate was missing altogether.

"What are you going to do next?" the photographer asked.

Rosa sat back in her chair and closed her eyes. That something had happened that shouldn't have happened was clear. She tried to arrive at some useful conclusion.

"Look. Sheriff Gonzalo has already started his investigation, I'm sure. He was there at the scene. He's visiting family in Rincón, and he should be back tomorrow. I say we hold these pictures until he gets here."

"I can't wait until tomorrow," said the photographer.

"Why not? The dead guy will still be dead."

"I will be too. They know who I am. The police know who I am."

"How do you know? You were hiding, weren't you?"

"Yes, but they found me. They know who I am, where I live, everything."

"What do you mean they found you?"

"The lieutenant gave me a ticket. He knows who I am."

"A ticket for what?"

"He found me behind the bushes. He gave me a ticket for trespassing. The beach is supposed to be closed at that hour."

"Did you give him your real name and—"

"Yes! I told you, they know who I am. They want the pictures. They want the negatives."

"Maybe it was just an honest ticket."

There was some need to justify the lieutenant's actions. No police officer wants to believe that a comrade is guilty of some serious offense, and it does not get much more serious than covering up a murder and silencing witnesses.

"If it was a good ticket, why were there four police officers at my door at six in the morning? They gave me a head start and followed me home. They showed me a badge: I said I had to go to the bathroom before I could let them in, then I grabbed my bag and ran out the back door into the woods. When they followed me into the woods, I circled back, got in my car and was gone before they could react. I was doing ninety on the road here."

"Wait a minute. At that speed it doesn't take more than two hours to get here. At that speed it doesn't even take one hour. Where were you?" Rosa asked. She couldn't act on an allegation this grave if there were holes in the photographer's story.

"I parked outside of town. I got out and hid in the bushes until a few minutes ago. Then I drove into town. I can't take chances. I'm not some Green Beret. I can't fight these guys; all I can do is run and hide. That's why I came to Gonzalo. He looked like the only honest cop on that beach. I need protection."

Rosa closed her eyes to think. Without some more tangible danger, there was no reason to interrupt Gonzalo's vacation. She wasn't sure she wanted to get Collazo from his pew. Still, she looked at her watch and knew the service would be over soon enough.

"Wait here a minute, okay? I'm gonna get another deputy. We'll figure out exactly what to do, okay?"

The photographer thought the proposition over for a moment and nodded her approval with reluctance. As Officer Almodovar crossed to the door, the young lady stopped her.

"Where are you from?" she asked.

"New York City. Why?"

"Were you a cop there?"

"There and in San Juan. I'm not a rookie. Why?"

"No reason. You have an accent, that's all."

The photographer turned back to the pictures she had taken and Rosa left the station house.

The officer was angry as she crossed the plaza, though she knew she had no real reason to be. Since moving to Puerto Rico she had often been made to feel like something less than Puerto Rican. Her Nuyorican accent told everyone who heard her that she had not grown up on the island and this was a strike against her. In New York, some had seen her as nothing but a Puerto Rican. In Puerto Rico, she wasn't Puerto Rican enough.

Inside the church, her mood did not improve. She was only a good enough Catholic to care that she wasn't a very good Catholic at all. She opened the church door and wondered how long it had been since her last confession. It came to her. She had confessed shooting down an armed suspect in her first year working in New York.

She knew she should not proceed into the church without having first blessed herself with the holy water, but she couldn't find any. In the vestibule there was a water fountain, but no font. In the church itself there was nothing attached to the walls, nothing in all the empty space behind the rows of pews, and nothing near the pillars at the rear of the church. With her luck, Collazo was seated in the second row, paying close attention to the priest and no attention to anything else.

Rosa left the church and reentered it, hoping to find the holy water on her second approach. No luck. She left and reentered again. On this entry, Collazo was walking down the center aisle coming toward her. All eyes were on him as he walked. At one of the pillars, he stopped to dip two fingers into a small half bowl built into it facing the altar. He crossed himself and whispered something his partner couldn't hear.

"The priest said you were acting strangely at the back of the church: I figured you wanted me," Collazo said once they were out on the plaza.

"Yeah, well, I've got a strange case for you. Just wait 'til you get to the station house," Rosa countered. She made a mental note to have Collazo show her around town during the daytime—no major building on her beat should be as great a mystery to her as the church had been.

There was no one waiting inside the station house. A search of the neighborhood revealed only that the photographer was not to be seen and that no one recalled her passing by.

The pictures were found in their envelope, locked away in Collazo's lap drawer, the magnifying glass resting on top. The negatives, like the woman who had developed them, were gone.

Chapter Nine

Gonzalo arrived in Angustias that Sunday at about one in the afternoon. He left Mari at his mother's house and after finding that nothing had happened since the last time he called, he left for the station house with a promise to return within the hour or call.

From the outside it appeared that the work on the precinct was nearing completion. While there was no smooth coating of cement on the cinder block addition, the walls themselves seemed complete. The wooden forms for the additional roofing were already up. Before entering, Gonzalo walked around to the side of the station house and found that bars had been installed already in the prisoner's windows. He was impressed, and told the workers as much as they filed back to the site from their lunch.

Inside, the deputies had arranged the two desks back to back, and there were two deputies seated at each table. Collazo sat with his partner and Hector sat beside his. Each officer had a magnifying glass and a handful of photos.

"What are you all looking at?" Gonzalo said when none of them looked at him.

"Hey, Chief," Hector said, instantly grating on Gonzalo's nerves with that phrase. "We're looking at murder here. One murder and it looks like a lot of natural causes. Mostly rocks, I figure."

"How do you know it's murder?" Gonzalo asked, pulling a chair out for himself.

"Son, somebody took a claw hammer or a crowbar to that boy's head," Collazo answered. "You can see the marking it left as plain as I can see you."

"And you're all positive it isn't just a strange mark from a rock?" Gonzalo pressed. He wanted to be positive this was a homicide before going forward with his investigation.

"Sir, with all due respect, I could believe it was a rock that made that hole in the guy's head, but no rock pulled his pockets out. Look at this picture: Somebody went through his pockets looking for something. You can tell from the picture where they're carrying him to the car that someone pulled out his back pockets, too," Rosa said. Each time she wanted to say the word *retrato*, she stumbled over its Rs and opted for the easier to pronounce *foto*.

Officer Calderon continued the analysis. "Also, you can tell from his tan that he had a watch at some point. Maybe he left it in Santo Domingo, but since his pockets were emptied, it's not unreasonable to assume the watch was stolen as well."

"Make any progress in identifying the victim?" Hector asked.

"None. It got worse."

"Worse than what?"

"Worse than not knowing who the victim is. Now nobody even knows where the body is. Those guys who put him in the trunk, that sergeant driving the car, they all seem to be part of a cover-up."

"Couldn't it be clerical?" Officer Calderon asked.

"What?"

"Couldn't they have just misplaced his paperwork?"

Gonzalo took the magnifying glass from her hand and went over the photos where the body was being carried to the car. After a minute of intense scrutiny, he gave his answer.

"Nope. See the tag on his wrist when he's on the beach? It's already missing when they carried him to the car. That's where the disposal of his body began. No clerical error. That body was just dumped, his tag assigned to the next victim."

One of the construction workers walked into the precinct. Outside, the screech and rumble of a big truck approaching was becoming audible, then deafening.

"They're ready, *señores, señoras*."

"Ready for what?" Gonzalo asked. He was more than a little upset that official police business no less serious than a murder investigation could be interrupted by construction work he didn't want and hadn't asked for.

"Ready to pour the cement," the worker said, and pointed at the wooden forms overhead.

"So go ahead," Gonzalo said.

"No, no. You can't be in here." The worker smiled.

"Why not?"

"If the wood breaks . . ." He pointed again at the wood forms.

Gonzalo was left to deduce that if the wood forms were unable to do their job, most of the Angustias police force would be buried under ten thousand pounds of wet concrete.

"Give us a few minutes to get our stuff, okay?" Gonzalo went to the gun locker and retrieved two shotguns and several boxes of ammunition. "Bring the pictures and the magnifying glasses," he said, and made his way to the door.

When his deputies got outside, the sheriff was adjusting one of the shotguns into an upright gun rack fitted between driver and passenger seats of the squad car. The other shotgun went into the squad car's trunk.

"What is this, the Alamo?" Collazo asked.

"We'll talk in Cafetin Lolita," Gonzalo said and the deputies followed him to a tiny diner a hundred yards away.

Cafetin Lolita was the only place near the center of Angustias that served a traditional Puerto Rican lunch. There was a pizzeria and a shop for teenagers that sold hamburgers and strange-colored slurpies. The grocery store made sandwiches (Gonzalo's usual lunch when at work) and there was a truck that sometimes came into town selling hot dogs and such. Cafetin Lolita sold real food—rice and beans with a large portion of some meat and a wedge of avocado was a typical lunch for Collazo, who was counted among the regular customers. With this, he drank a tall glass of iced water—he wouldn't have had a beer or a glass of wine while on duty even if it could save his life.

The diner was empty when the officers arrived, and Lolita Gomez, the owner, came out from the back.

"What do you want?" she asked, somewhat testily. She wasn't asking about their orders. Instead, it appeared that she had been rocking in a hammock in the back and disturbed in her sleep.

Collazo ignored her mood and asked for his favorite meal. She took out an order pad and a pen. The other officers followed Collazo's lead except for Rosa, who was looking in a menu that looked older than she was.

"*Ay Virgen. Mi'ja*, that menu was printed when President Kennedy was killed. God rest his soul, he died a good Catholic." Lolita crossed herself and kissed her thumb, presenting it to heaven.

"Then why do you keep it around?" Rosa asked out of curiosity.

Lolita laughed at the display of ignorance. "Have you ever seen a restaurant without a menu?" she asked quite sensibly. "Don't look at the menu, just tell me what you want."

"Can I get a cheeseburger?"

"No."

"Plain hamburger?"

"No."

"Hotdog with—"

"No."

"Turkey and bacon on rye?"

"Bacon, yes. Turkey, no. Rye, like whiskey?"

"Give me what Officer Calderon is having."

"And to drink?"

"Pepsi?"

"Coke."

"Diet?"

"What?"

126

"Coke is fine."

As Lolita flicked her notepad closed, Rosa could see the page was still as blank as it had been before the ordering started. The pen had never been uncapped.

"You didn't write anything down," Rosa pointed out as Lolita was turning to go back behind the counter.

"What do you want me to write?" Lolita asked. It had apparently never dawned on her that the order pad might be used to record orders.

"The orders!" Rosa insisted as her fellow officers began to laugh at her.

"Why? You going to forget?" Lolita asked.

Rosa could see that further inquiry into Lolita's business practices would be fruitless, but she couldn't help asking a final question. "Why do you even have the pad if you're not going to write in it?"

Lolita laughed again as though the young lady before her could not have asked a stranger question. "This girl's never been to a restaurant before in her life, right?" she asked no one in particular, then she walked away.

No one came in to interrupt the police business that was conducted over the food.

Gonzalo spoke first. "Where's that other guy?" he asked.

"What other guy, Chief?" Hector responded.

"The new deputy, what's his name?"

"Abel? He's on a split shift like you said. He won't start again until three."

"Has he seen the pictures?"

"No. Want me to get them over to him?"

"It can wait. What needs to be done won't get done on a Sunday, I'm pretty sure. I'll talk to him when he comes in."

Collazo spoke next. "We need to speak to that sergeant and those other officers."

Officer Calderon agreed. "If they covered up the murder, then they know who did it. There's no other reason to dump the body."

Gonzalo thought a moment before speaking.

"I agree, but there's a small problem maybe Fernandez can help with. I think the officers taking the body away came out of a precinct in San Juan. Nobody else sent officers. Clearly you, Rosa, don't recognize any of these faces." He waited for her response as she took another look at the photos.

"Never seen any of them. I put in my two years in La Perla. Didn't get to see many officers except the ones in my precinct."

La Perla is one of the toughest neighborhoods on the island. It's built outside the walls of Old San Juan on the ocean's edge. From the right angles, the houses, many made of scrap wood and corrugated zinc panels, seem to be gripping the ragged rock face at the shore the way terns cling to oceanside cliffs. While many of the inhabitants are decent people of the poorest stripe, the neighborhood is infested with violent criminals, drug offenders, and prostitutes. Police officers are posted at the entrances to the neighborhood twenty-four hours a day, keeping tourists from wandering in.

"You worked in La Perla?" Officer Calderon asked with surprise in her voice, as though Rosa had mentioned walking on the moon.

"I got this in La Perla," Rosa said using her fork to point to a six-inch scar along the underside of her jawline. "And this." She pointed to similar scars cutting across the flesh near her right elbow. "That was a bad night," Rosa said and continued her eating.

It was Gonzalo who brought the conversation back to the topic at hand. "What about the photographer? If she was afraid of these policemen, maybe she had dealt with them before."

"Well, I can vouch for her being afraid, there's no doubt about that. But she left no clue where she might have run to, and I'm sure she wasn't headed home again," Rosa added.

"Well, I'll go home and make some phone calls to Rincón about her," Gonzalo said. "For now, I want you and Collazo to go home and get some rest. I'll swing by to see Officer Fernandez and talk to him about the photos. He worked in San Juan; maybe he knows one of the guys we're looking for. There might be crooked cops out there, so be careful."

The officers got ready to bus their table, but Officer Calderon held up her hand to get the attention of the others. "I just want to point out one thing before we accept the theory that these cops are behind a murder. This guy in the photo was killed on board the ship before it sank. It seems more than possible that whoever killed him also wound up on the beach face up in the sand. Maybe he was the captain and he got into an argument with a passenger, or vice versa. These cops may have had very good reasons for carrying out the body this way. Just because we can't think of these reasons now doesn't mean they don't exist."

It was a sobering thought, that they might be investigating, harassing even, good cops just trying to do their jobs. Gonzalo considered his response.

"They threatened my daughter over the phone. If these are good cops, they don't look like it to me. Let's not lose focus. I want us to do our jobs and get to the bottom of things no matter where we have to go for this. Understood?"

Hector knew as much as Gonzalo had revealed to him, but the other officers had no idea what type of personal stake their sheriff had in the matter. Collazo followed him out of the diner.

"Son, wait for me. Now these guys, they said what about your child?"

Gonzalo stopped on the narrow sidewalk outside of Cafetin Lolita and looked at his old friend.

"They called me in Rincón to tell me to stop investigating and to let me know they were watching my daughter. They never mentioned physical harm, but it was implied. Without any question in my mind."

Collazo put his hand on Gonzalo's shoulder. "If you want me to, I can drive Mari and little Sonia to a safe place. I have family in Ponce."

"I want them where I can keep an eye on them. Mari wouldn't go for it anyway."

Collazo shrugged. While it was his place to offer assistance, it was not his place to insist, though he was thirty years older than his sheriff and as close a friend as Gonzalo had. In Collazo's philosophy, each man had to be allowed to do what he thought best for his family.

"Now let me call Mari to tell her I'm coming home." Gonzalo went to the pay phone at the end of the block and called his wife to tell her he would be stopping at Abel Fernandez's home for a moment before coming to her. Then he called Fernandez. As he expected, the officer had no objections to seeing him before work. Nor did he express any particular desire to see the sheriff. This also was as Gonzalo expected.

Fernandez rented an apartment on top of the auto repair shop run by Domingo Ramos. There was one large room that served Fernandez as both living room and bedroom, and there was a kitchen and a bathroom. The furnishings consisted of only the most essential pieces—a bed neatly made, two chairs placed by a card table, a radio on a shelf. There was only one decorative element in the large room—a single red plastic rose sat in a sturdy, clear long stem vase; it was of the type that gathers dust in the cheapest of restaurants.

When Gonzalo knocked, Fernandez shuffled to the door and opened, saying nothing and not smiling, only waving Gonzalo out of the sun and fresh air.

"How can I help you?" he asked Gonzalo.

"Well, it's very simple really. I just need to see if you recognize any of the officers in these photos."

Gonzalo pulled the photos out of their manila envelope and handed them one by one to Fernandez. He watched his deputy closely for a facial reaction, but Fernandez did nothing to hide his unease.

"These cops are from San Juan," Gonzalo pointed out.

"I know them. I'm here because I want nothing to do with them. Where'd you get these pictures?"

"Never mind where I got the pictures."

"The photographer'll be dead before he makes it off the island. If you talk to him again, tell him not to head for the airport."

"What do you mean?"

Abel sat on his bed and looked at the pictures even more closely.

"I mean these are bad people you have on film here. Walk away from them. Whatever they did, leave it be. Believe me. It's better that way."

"I'm investigating the murder and disappearance of the man you see them carrying there. I can't just walk away from that," Gonzalo pointed out.

Fernandez handed the photos back and crossed his arms. "Walk away. I walked away from these guys every time they pulled one of their stunts. It's easy, all the cops in El Condado precinct do it; at least the guys from my shift. When they beat a prisoner, look somewhere else. When they mention the word 'bury,' stop listening. When they ask you what you saw or what you heard, say 'huh?'"

"They threatened my family," Gonzalo answered.

"It's not an idle threat. You remember Sergeant Santiago Cruz? Do you really think drug dealers killed him in a crossfire?

"They kill whoever they want. Remember Officer Otero a few months ago? You honestly believe Colombian druglords came all the way to Puerto Rico to tie him up and shoot him in the back of the head? Why? Otero was a rookie. Never made more than a few nickel and dime drug busts."

"Is any of this fact, or are you guessing?"

"Are you asking as a sheriff?"

"I'm just a man who needs to get a little information."

"Fact. But I wouldn't testify to any of it. Look. I spent my last few years in San Juan just walking away from these guys and everything they did. I walked so much, I wound up in this little town which I had never even heard of. I suggest you do exactly the same."

"That's a coward's way out," Gonzalo said. He was more than a little upset with his new deputy's attitude. More importantly, he didn't like the way the conversation was making him have second thoughts.

Fernandez shrugged his shoulders. "I didn't say it was noble; I just say it's a way out. Coward, brave, those are just words."

"Can I just have the names of the officers you recognize?"

"Sure. This is Officer Rios, Jaime, I think. Nice guy, except when he's on the job. This one's Officer Rivera, Edwin. Mean, always. That's Sergeant Ochoa, Nestor. He leads the guys in the field;

don't know where he gets his orders from, but the captain at El Condado rubber-stamps everything. Watch out for Ochoa—between him and the Devil there's only a shade of difference, and I can't tell which is better. Ochoa would kill his own mother without losing sleep, and he'd kill yours for fun."

"Who's the lieutenant?" Gonzalo asked.

Fernandez took the photo back into his hands and studied it. "Can't help you there. Never saw him. Not from El Condado."

Gonzalo took the photos back and put them all into the envelope, then he looked at his deputy sitting on his bed. The man was clearly damaged goods. Fernandez returned his stare.

"You want me to leave your precinct, just let me know. I'll transfer out."

Gonzalo looked to his shoes for the right answer. He prided himself in being a calm, reasonable man, but the news from Fernandez was disturbing. He wasn't sure what he thought of his deputy. He had come to Angustias for a fresh start, but Gonzalo wasn't sure he could wipe the deputy's slate clean and trust him.

"Just tell me one thing. If these guys come to town, if they come after my wife or my daughter or me, are you just going to walk away?"

"I don't know. I'll tell you when they get here," Fernandez said quietly.

"Not good enough. I'll fill out the transfer

forms tomorrow morning. Let me know where you want to go; you'll be there in a week."

Fernandez only nodded and shrugged as the sheriff made his way out.

Later that night, in an interrogation room in the El Condado precinct three officers gathered to discuss plans concerning Sheriff Gonzalo. Specifically, they devised a plot by which they would be certain Gonzalo would take his attention from the cover-up of a murder. After much debate, they decided on two plans, one no less outrageous than the other, the second to be implemented in the event the first plan met with failure.

In all their planning, their voices never became heated. They had been successful in similar projects; in fact, this was far from difficult in their estimation. Difficult had been the assassination of one mayoral candidate at a rally, in front of a crowd and the media. Another candidate in that race was implicated, indicted, and convicted in that murder and was awaiting word on an appeal.

It was further decided by the three (of whom Sergeant Ochoa was the lowest in rank) that Gonzalo would be given one last chance to end his investigation. One last phone call would be made to warn him off the case. If he refused to listen to reason, the fury of Hell would be let loose on Angustias as a diversion.

Chapter Ten

Gonzalo did not get a threatening phone call. Sergeant Ochoa was supposed to handle that call, one among the many details required by the plans to disrupt Gonzalo's investigation. One particular part of the plan, the selection of men he would lead in the field, took much longer than he thought it would, and Sergeant Ochoa fell asleep on a sofa in the officer's lounge. He dreamt that he found Gonzalo sleeping in his uniform under a tall palm tree. In the dream, Ochoa raised a television set over his head and threw it down on Gonzalo with all the strength he could muster. He was about to check whether his victim had survived or died when the precinct clerk shook him awake.

"Sergeant Ochoa? Sergeant Ochoa! You have a call waiting for you."

Ochoa stumbled his way to his desk. During the night, he had crooked one leg beneath the other and tucked his left arm beneath his head. Both of these limbs were in a profound sleep.

"Is this Sergeant Nestor Ochoa?"

"Yes. Who's this?" Ochoa asked, but he recognized the voice as he was forming the words.

"This is Sheriff Luis Gonzalo from Angustias. You may not remember me, but we spoke on the beach . . ." Gonzalo paused.

"You're right, I don't remember you." That wasn't exactly what Ochoa had wanted to say. He wanted to say he hadn't been to a beach in months, but he was still too sleepy, and the right words refused to come in time.

"Well, I was at Las Puntas in Rincón the other night when you came to help out with the shipwreck. We have photographs of you and your men on the beach. I'm trying to track down one of the bodies that washed up on the beach: a young man, white shirt, light beige pants, hole in the back of his head . . ."

"Doesn't ring a bell."

"That's funny. The pictures show you watching as your men put him in a squad car trunk. Then we have a clear shot of you driving that car off."

Sergeant Ochoa had terminated the phone call on his end. He then made several phone calls of his own and drove home. It was a little before ten by the time he had changed into the appropriate civilian clothing, and it was a little past ten-thirty when he met with men in two cars in the parking lot of the Arecibo shopping mall by the sea.

"You men know the plan?" he asked, still in the driver's seat of a car he had chosen for this project.

"Lieutenant told us everything we need to know."

"You have everything you need for this job?"

One of the men pulled up the sweatshirt he was wearing: He had on a bulletproof vest. "Everything and a little more," he said with a smile.

One of the others spoke up. "Let me just get straight on two things: A—We finish this job and we walk away, no strings, no lawyers, nothing; just drive out and keep driving."

"No strings except one," the sergeant answered. "You get caught, for this or any other thing, I will put you down like a dog."

"That's cool. I got a plane ticket already. But B—Anything we grab is ours, no meeting to split anything, strictly cash and carry, right?"

"You get it, it's yours. You pick up a toaster, it's yours; you pick up a million dollars, it's yours. You get greedy and decide to spend more time in that town than I have planned for, I will kill you and go. You all understand that part? Any of you mess this thing up for me, you will not live to see the sunset. Let's be clear on that."

The men nodded their agreement and got into their respective cars. Two men climbed in with Sergeant Ochoa. They made a stop at a phone bank before leaving the mall parking lot, and Ochoa made two phone calls. They were on the road to Angustias before the clock had struck eleven.

While Ochoa was making preparations for a grand entrance into Angustias, Gonzalo continued to make phone calls to a variety of offices, each successful in its own way in keeping him from imparting or receiving any useful information about the case at hand.

His first call was to the office of the Chief of Police in San Juan. The chief wasn't in, his assistant said. The deputy chiefs were in different meetings, but they would all be glad to get back to him if he cared to leave a message. He left a message with each chief that said the same thing: "Sgt. Nestor Ochoa. Las Puntas, Rincón." His idea was to see which of the chiefs understood the message.

The next call was to the Immigration and Naturalization Service, where he got a recording at first. When he reached a live voice, it was that of a junior official who said, "We only really care about the live ones. The dead ones get repatriated

140

sooner or later, but it's not like we can interview them or anything. They don't make any claims for asylum. Not really our job." He was about to hang up.

"But one of them was murdered," Gonzalo said, raising his voice.

The official laughed out loud. "Call the FBI. I'm sure they'll make it a top priority. Good day, sheriff." He hung up, and the last thing Gonzalo heard was unstifled laughter.

Gonzalo did call the FBI's office in San Juan. After spending twenty minutes on hold, he got through to an agent who seemed to be eating a late breakfast while listening to Gonzalo's predicament.

"What would you like me to do, Sheriff?"

"Well, I'm talking about the murder of a citizen of the Dominican Republic which happened on our shores. I expect you might be able to begin some sort of investigation."

"Are you willing to accept FBI assistance on an investigation you are currently pursuing?"

Gonzalo was excited by this prospect. It seemed to be the answer to a great many problems he had gotten into over this investigation. "Yes. That's exactly what I want. Yes. Good."

"All right. I will see what I can do on my end. I'll make a few calls, do a little snooping, but let me tell you: local authorities should really be do-

141

ing most of the work on this, at least the beginning. Now tell me what you have on the victim. Hold on, let me get another pencil."

Gonzalo began by giving a description of the corpse and the injury to the head.

"Whoa, whoa, whoa. I meant more like his name, where he lived. More importantly, where's the body now? San Juan morgue? Ponce?"

Gonzalo had none of this information.

"You don't have a body? What kind of murder case do you intend to build without a body? Pictures of a body? Look, I can't help you. A picture of a dead body on a beach with twenty or thirty other dead bodies isn't much to go on. If you get anything else—"

Gonzalo interrupted. "I think there is evidence of a police cover-up. There are pictures of officers taking the body, stuffing it into the trunk of a squad car with no license plates and driving off."

"Take it to your department's Internal Affairs, sheriff." The agent hung up.

Gonzalo sat for a moment with the receiver in his hands. In all his years, he had not heard of the IA office doing anything but bumbling their way through cases, keeping secret information that should have been public, and, more importantly, making public information that should never have seen the light of day. They let cops who were more plainly guilty than Satan go free and made up for this by ruining the careers and lives of cops who had done nothing or little wrong. Only rookies and the truly desperate went to IA. He wondered how truly desperate he was.

His daughter walked by him, and he decided to take a chance on IA. The recorded message at their offices told him that the normal recorded message was out of order. There would therefore be no buttons for him to push to redirect his call.

Mari came up from behind him and put a hand on his shoulder. "It's eleven o'clock. Either get ready to go to work or help me grind some coffee for the rest of the week."

Gonzalo looked at his wife, considered his options and headed for the shower.

By the time he got out of the shower and had dressed himself, Mari had ground enough coffee for the rest of the week and was peeling an orange for Sonia at the kitchen table. Sonia was singing a song taught to first graders to help them remember key words in English—"*Ventura*, window; *y piso*, floor."

In the first instant, before they realized he was looking at them, the women in his life seemed pure and beautiful to him. When they turned to face him, however, he could think nothing but that they were vulnerable.

"Mari," he called his wife. She finished peeling the orange, cut it in half, and handed it to Sonia before going to where he stood.

"I'm getting a bad feeling about this investigation I'm doing. I think I'm dealing with some people who are very bad. Here is the key to the lockbox." He took a small key off his key chain. "When was the last time you practiced?" he asked.

"I don't know. You're scaring me. What did you hear in those phone calls you made?"

"Nothing. I heard that we're on our own. Look, just remember this: Don't let Sonia go outside without you; someone comes in here without your invitation, shoot them—don't threaten, don't negotiate, just pull the trigger. Aim for the chest; keep the gun pointed wherever your eyes are looking. Come on; watch me load the gun."

Gonzalo took down the lockbox from the closet shelf in their room and opened it on the bureau. He loaded the .38 with six rounds and made sure Mari saw the twelve other rounds pointing to the sky from their slots in the box. He handed the gun to his wife.

"Crack it open . . . Good. Snap it shut . . . Good. Aim at the window . . . Good. Aim at the mirror . . . Good, you turned with your shoulders. Now aim at my head."

Mari began the turn to follow his instructions, but decided to aim at the ceiling instead.

"Very good. You are wise beyond your years, young grasshopper," Gonzalo said, imitating the Shaolin priest from the TV show *Kung Fu*.

"I'll leave my car CB on. You know the police frequency. You have any trouble here, don't hesitate. Get on the CB and send out an SOS. I'll tell the off-duty officers to carry their radios with them."

He kissed Mari good-bye and climbed into his car, turning on his CB as promised. While the car warmed and his wife went back into the house, he studied the absolute blueness of the sky, and he trained his thoughts on the uncleared woods near his house, hoping to be able to pick out some sound. There were crickets and a single tree frog making their distinctive sounds. He had been too busy of late to clear away the underbrush near the house. There were insects and animals in there that had no idea yet that the sun had come out, though it was now climbing high into the sky. He'd have to get in there with a machete and release the crickets from their bondage to darkness.

There was nothing on the radio until he had already pulled away from the house. His wife got to him when he had already rounded a long curve headed towards the center of town.

"Luis? Pick up."

"What's the matter, Mari?"

"Your new deputy, Fernandez, just called. He said he saw the sergeant from the pictures drive into town. He says he thinks there was another car. He thinks a total of six, possibly seven men."

"Where were they headed?"

"Straight to town."

"Did Fernandez say anything else?"

"Yeah. He said he was packing."

Gonzalo banged the CB against his forehead several times, muttering all sorts of convoluted curses against Fernandez for his cowardice, and against Sergeant Ochoa for his steel-faced boldness. "Mari, keep that gun handy and lock yourself in the house. Don't open for anyone but me, you understand?"

"The gun's in my hand right now. What are you going to do?"

"I'm going to have a talk with this Ochoa. I'll be in town in three minutes."

"Be careful, Luis."

"Always."

Gonzalo had pushed the gas pedal to floor when he heard of Ochoa's presence in Angustias. He was doing eighty-five miles an hour on a road filled with sharp turns. Three minutes was an outside estimate.

He was less than a minute from the center of

town when the CB came to life again. It was Officer Iris Calderon.

"Hector, are you there?" she called, fear obvious in her voice. "Hector, are you there? There's a bank robbery in progress. Oh my God! They're coming out. Hector, are you there?"

"I'm coming. Do not confront the robbers," Gonzalo answered her calmly. He was thirty seconds from the bank, which was on a side street off the plaza.

"I repeat. Do not confront them," Gonzalo stressed.

The reply he heard on the open channel was deafening. There was the murderous clanging of rapid-fire shots careening off parts of the squad car. Someone was using an Uzi or an AK-47 or something. There were the screams of dozens if not hundreds of people and the sound of Iris Calderon firing her standard issue six-shooter. The CB noise was numbing. Gonzalo imagined Officer Calderon trapped in her car, her gun in one hand, the CB in the other, keeping the channel open, with a deadly tight grip on both.

The CB picked up every explosion. It picked up the windshield bursting under assault rifle force; the thud of lead hitting the dash and padded leather seats. It picked up Iris yelling "Shit!" a dozen times and "I got one!" and "He got me!" in a tone filled with more annoyance than pain. It picked up Rosa Almodovar telling Iris help was on the way.

Gonzalo slammed on the brakes the moment he entered town. The streets near the plaza were cluttered with mothers racing to find children who were running in a panic of unmitigated terror. Men were crouched behind cars; a few lay flat on their bellies in the middle of the street. Gonzalo could see one, no, two, no, three people dripping blood as they walked, dazed, from the direction of the bank. The sounds from the CB were increased by the ambient noise.

Gonzalo got out of the car. It was less than a hundred yards to the bank, but he had to wade through the crowds, and they were determined to go in the opposite direction. The last census had shown only a few more than nine thousand citizens in Angustias, and it seemed that they were all blocking his path. He drew his gun as he rounded the corner and the bank came into view. This street was almost completely deserted except for the robbers, Officer Calderon and a few civilians trying to crawl their way to safety.

The squad car was parked directly in front of the bank. Iris Calderon was crouched beside it, keeping the car between her and the two masked men who were pumping round after round from AK-47's into the car in short bursts, as though there were some magic number of bullets needed to kill Deputy Calderon.

Gonzalo ran toward the scene at full speed. He could see she was trying to reload her weapon from the bullets at the back of her gunbelt. She was effectively pinned down. As long as the AK-47's had bullets she would be a fool to show her face, let alone take effective aim.

Gonzalo kept running.

He could see also three bodies on the ground in front of the bank. One of them seemed to be a bank robber; the others were people from town, *Angustiados*.

He kept running.

He could see Officer Almodovar running from further down the street. Her gun was out, and Collazo was running at his best speed, weapon drawn, behind her. Hector was coming from the direction of the plaza at his best speed, his non-standard .45 in hand. His arms were pumping. He jumped over a parked motorcycle like others might step over a crack in the sidewalk. One of the gunmen began to move around the side of the squad car toward Calderon, who could not see him coming and could hear no shouts of warning above the sound of her car's destruction.

Gonzalo kept running, coming to a range where his shots might be effective, raising his weapon.

He saw two other gunmen waiting, watching from the bank's doorway. One gunman was now only five feet from Officer Calderon. He raised his AK-47 to eye level and took careful aim. Calderon noticed his shadow on her and fell from her haunches to her butt. Gonzalo stopped in mid-run and aimed at the man's torso. He pulled the trigger twice. The man turned around, his eyes looking for whoever had shot him in the back. He found Gonzalo. Gonzalo fired two more rounds. The man staggered a step back and raised his weapon again. Hector fired five rounds in quick succession. Everyone heard the thud of these bullets hitting the man, but he did not lower his weapon. Iris Calderon snapped shut her service revolver and fired a round into his ass. He dropped his gun and fell like an axed tree.

Rosa Almodovar ran into the fray and brought her weapon to eye level, aiming at the second AK-47 man. She yelled "Freeze!" in English several times, and when he turned to her, his gun still raised, she emptied her revolver into his chest. He fell straight back, as people do when they've been hypnotized by a magician. She cracked open her gun and reached for her rapid reload as one of the gunmen in the doorway stepped out toward her with a pump action shotgun in hand.

Hector did not see this second gunman: instead he was hurrying to the side of his partner.

Gonzalo saw him, but was distracted because he recognized the gunman still in the doorway; it was Sgt. Ochoa. Collazo saw the threat to his partner and stopped in his tracks some ten yards behind Almodovar, taking careful aim above her head, trying to find a spot right between the eyes of the bank thief.

Another gunman showed himself at the bank doorway. Officer Almodovar had not yet reloaded. The gunman took aim, she knelt to avoid him; he aimed again; she snapped shut her weapon and rolled to avoid his aim. He took aim again; she fired without aim—she fired out of fear, out of terror—he fired calmly and took a part of her skull right behind her right ear cleanly off her head. The gunman stopped moving a moment to admire his work, and Collazo found the target he wanted and pulled the trigger. The gunman stood with a dark spot directly above his right eye for a second before dropping. Collazo maintains to this day that the gunman changed his focus to look him in the face with bewilderment in his eyes.

Another gunman stepped from the doorway of the bank and pumped a round from his shotgun in Collazo's general direction. Gonzalo watched as his seventy-seven-year-old deputy spun in place and fell to the sidewalk sitting, holding his hip. Gonzalo fired two more shots to empty his gun into this gunman's back, but his bullets had only the effect of making the gunman turn towards him.

Hector stood from his position beside Officer Calderon and raised his gun hand over the hood of the squad car in a fluid motion, the gun a mere extension of his hand, finding the target he wanted with the ease others used to point a finger at a mountain. He pulled the trigger once, and Gonzalo can still recall clearly the split second after the man's knees hit the sidewalk and before his blood and bits of brain splattered to the ground.

Gonzalo jumped back to a position behind the battered squad car, near Officer Calderon. With a quick glance he could tell she had been hit in her left leg, a few inches above her ankle. Her face was covered with scratches, probably from her windshield glass.

Gonzalo rapidly reloaded his .38. When he looked up, Hector was no longer near, Sgt. Ochoa was no longer in the doorway, and the man Rosa Almodovar had brought down to the ground was struggling to his knees, his AK-47 still in hand.

Gonzalo sprang out from behind the squad car and made eye contact with this gunman, but he couldn't tell in that moment what the assailant was thinking, so he raised his handgun and put two bullets in his head. If you ask Gonzalo now what he thinks of that moment, he will say he thinks the gunman's eyes were filled with nothing more than dazed confusion. Still, he will say it was a good shoot because he is sure he did not see surrender in the gunman's eyes. Then he will turn away and change the subject, asking you not to bring up that day again.

Gonzalo heard a shotgun blast and found Hector and Sergeant Ochoa. Ochoa was in the driver's seat of a medium-sized brown car, perhaps a Nova. Another bank robber was backing his way into the open passenger-side door. He held an elderly woman as a shield. Hector was walking towards the gunman, his gun upraised, one eye closed, the other squinting along the gun barrel, fury written plainly in every muscle of his face. Gonzalo watched his deputy and the gunman. He knew Hector could easily pick a spot on the man's forehead and open a hole in it. He knew Hector was using all the restraint at his command not to pull the trigger.

The gunman sat in the passenger seat, and Ochoa floored the accelerator. As they turned the corner a hundred feet away, the old woman was thrown to the street and the passenger door closed.

"After them! After them!" Gonzalo yelled. Hector turned to him, and Gonzalo pointed at a row of parked motorcycles. Hector looked closely at several, found the keys still in the ignition of one of them, hopped on, gunned the motor, and sped away in pursuit. Gonzalo turned to the sea of wounded and dead around him.

"Call an ambulance!" he yelled out to no one in particular, unaware that there was no one left on that street in any condition to do anything he asked.

Chapter Eleven

The moment he saw Hector disappear around the corner on the motorcycle, Gonzalo was sorry he had sent the young man in pursuit. The sheriff liked to have enough time to make rational decisions. With only a few extra seconds, he realized he might have just sent a fine young officer on a suicide mission. In the next moment he realized that there might be other gunmen still in the bank.

"Is it over?" Officer Calderon asked. She was still sitting next to the squad car, her gun lying in the street by her hand. Her tone was one of utter exhaustion.

"Not by a long shot," Gonzalo said. "You'll be all right, but keep that gun in your hand. I'll be back in a second."

Gonzalo ran over to Collazo, crouching low as he went in case another gunman showed himself.

"How you doing, old man?"

"Not too good, son. I can't stand up."

"What do you mean?" Gonzalo asked, but he was already looking at his deputy's back, checking for a spinal injury.

"It hurts," Collazo answered, sounding very much like a frightened child.

"Will you be all right here until the ambulance comes?"

"Sure. I'll be fine. Go do what you have to do."

"I'm going to check on Rosa—"

"She's dead," Collazo said, as he lifted his hand part of the way off his wound and took a first look at the damage done to him.

Gonzalo walked towards Rosa Almodovar, his crouch less pronounced now. The force of the shotgun blast to her head had knocked her flat on her back. Time seemed to stop or slow as Gonzalo neared the corpse. He didn't notice the pool of blood on the sidewalk until he had knelt in it. He checked her neck for a pulse, and, not finding one, he turned her head to look for a wound.

The mess at the back of Rosa's head was profound. There was a flap of skin with bits of bone. Blood with small flecks of brain spilled when Gonzalo turned the head. A wave of nausea swept over the sheriff and he turned the head back to the face up position. After a moment used to compose himself by looking around and in through the bank door, he studied Rosa's face. There was no calm in Rosa's countenance. Her brow was furrowed with anger, her eyes were still open, the flesh around her mouth seemed to hang on her face, loose now that nothing at the back of her head restrained it; this made it seem as though Gonzalo could easily lift the death mask from her face and reveal the living woman. He was tempted to straighten her arms and holster the gun she still clutched. He wanted to button her collar and find the tie officers wore in formal settings, but all of this would be tampering with evidence that might someday be needed in court. There would be pictures of the body and a chalk outline. It could turn out to be the last case in which she testified. He closed her eyes and promised her a prayer.

He checked his gun and reloaded the two empty chambers, then looked up and down the street. There was a man inching his way around the corner, hugging the side of a building as he came. Gonzalo watched him and noticed a grimace on his face. He thought at first that the man had been wounded. Then he saw he was holding a broomstick. The grimace was the symbol of a great battle to win out against cold-hearted fear.

"Call an ambulance! Call the hospital in Ponce!" Gonzalo shouted to the man, waving him back.

"Which hospital?" the man wanted to know.

"All of them!"

"Do you want the police?"

Gonzalo thought a moment. Having just done battle with one part of Puerto Rico's police force, he wondered who he could trust.

"Call the sheriff of Naranjito. She's closest."

The man went back around the corner. It entered Gonzalo's mind that the broomstick would have been almost as effective as the shots he had fired.

"Sheriff!" Calderon called, and he went around to her side of the squad car.

"It's for you." She handed him her CB microphone and looked away.

"Luis, Luis, Luis." His wife was crying hysterically.

Gonzalo turned away from his young deputy. He had never heard his wife so thoroughly traumatized. She was sobbing over the CB; she had heard everything on her end. He wanted to cry in sympathy. His eyes welled with tears, a lump formed in his throat, and he wanted to get into a car and drive home to present himself to her as evidence that nothing had happened.

"I'm okay, Mari. I'm fine. I'm alive. I'm still standing. I am not hurt. Nothing happened to me. There's been a shootout. There's a big mess here, but I'm fine, okay?"

It took another minute of reassurances from

Gonzalo for Mari to calm to the point where she could say anything—and even then there was a hard sob between each word.

"Are . . . are . . . are . . . you . . . you . . . you . . . tell . . . ing . . . me . . . me . . . me . . . the . . . truth?"

"Mari. Believe me. Do you want me to sing for you?" He laughed.

"Yes," she sobbed, and he knew she was serious.

He sang the first lines of the Star-Spangled Banner as robustly as he could. Mari was satisfied.

"I'm . . . I'm . . . coming over there," she said, sniffling.

"Don't. Stay in the house. It's more dangerous now than before."

"I . . . I . . . I have to see you," Mari said.

"Call Sheriff Molina in Comerio. Tell him you need him to come over. Have him stay with you until I come home."

"I have to see you," Mari said, more forcefully.

"Don't open the door to anyone but Molina."

"I'm coming over—"

"Obey me!" Gonzalo shouted.

Mari was quiet a moment. She had not heard those words since her wedding day when she had agreed to do just what he now asked. She did not like it, and it made her cry again, but she agreed.

"I'll stop by as soon as I can, but I have one dead officer, two wounded officers and another officer, Hector, chasing the suspects. I've got dead and wounded suspects and civilians. It is a mess here, Mari. It looks like a bomb just went off. Clear this channel. Call Molina. I'll come by in an hour or two, okay?"

"Be careful," Mari said.

"I'm already careful," Gonzalo replied. "It's Sergeant Ochoa who needs to be careful now."

Gonzalo tossed the CB microphone onto Calderon's lap.

"How you holding up, kid?" he asked her.

"Anyone you want me to call on this?" she answered.

"Call anyone but the Metropolitan Police. Call Naranjito, advise them of our situation."

"Will do. Oh, Chief," she called him as he began to turn away. "Check your arm. You're hit."

Gonzalo glanced at his clean right arm and then to his bloody left arm. A bullet had gone cleanly through the muscle in his upper arm. Another bullet had grazed deeply into the forearm flesh near his left elbow. Both wounds were bleeding profusely and would need to be stitched. But that would wait until there was time. For now, he had others to tend to.

He checked first on the people on the sidewalk. He could find a pulse on none of them. The two civilians were known to him—Don Roberto DeJesus, Sr., a man nearly seventy years of age.

He owned a small farm on the outskirts of town and had come to the bank once a week for as long as Gonzalo could remember. Don Roberto had three holes in his thin chest; each wound had bled a little.

The other civilian was Doña Augustina De La Cruz, nearly sixty years of age. She was strictly religious, a Protestant. She came to the bank to do treasury chores for her church. A black leather Bible accompanied her everywhere, and it was clutched under her arm even in death. A bullet had pierced her neck, and she had sprayed her life out upon the sidewalk before Gonzalo even arrived on the scene. Her right hand was covered with blood, as though she had tried to stop its flow out of her, or perhaps she had tried to swat the mosquito she thought had just bit her.

Gonzalo walked into the bank, his gun in hand hanging down his right side. Three feet to the right of the door lay the guard, the hole of a shotgun blast where his heart should have been. Benji Carreras was eighteen; Gonzalo had helped to get him the job when he graduated from high school only a half-year before; he was saving for college. He had carried no gun, filling a role created more for form's sake than any other reason. The bank in Angustias was forty years old and had not had a moment's trouble in that time.

The other people in the bank, four customers

and four workers, were all on the floor, belly down, with their hands on the back of their heads. They were all fine, but had apparently been told not to get up until they had counted to a thousand very slowly. Though the shooting had been over for several minutes, they were not curious about who had won the gunfight. They did not lift their heads until Gonzalo had told them several times that it was all right to do so.

Raul Mendez, the bank manager, rushed to Gonzalo's side. He was a chubby, balding man who acted a bit effeminate because he thought that was a sign of style and taste.

"They took forty-two thousand dollars. There were seven of them. I counted. They took forty-two thousand dollars."

"They killed Benji," Gonzalo said, pointing his gun at the boy.

Mendez looked at the body and took a step towards it.

"*Ay, Cristo,*" he said, bringing his hand to his lips. "*Ay, Virgen*. Is he hurt bad?" Turning to Gonzalo.

"Nope. He's dead. Dead as hell."

"*Ay, Dios mío*. I heard a shot in here. My ears are still ringing. I thought they were shooting at the camera. That makes sense. The boy was getting on his belly. I watched him. He was crouching down like everyone else."

"You say there's a camera?"

"Right there, like always." Raul pointed to a corner of the room where several plastic plants hid a small black camera.

The camera was hidden from view unless you were near the teller's counter, then it had a clear view of the transaction. Gonzalo had been coming to this bank all his adult life and had never noticed the camera.

"How long has that been there?" he asked.

"Umm, maybe eight years. I can find out for sure if you want," Raul offered.

"Is it working?" Gonzalo asked. Many storeowners bought such equipment but did not maintain it. Keeping surveillance equipment in a visible location was thought to ward off thieves.

"Of course it's working," Raul said, with some injury in his voice.

"Good. Take out the tape and put it in the safe until I come for it, okay?"

"The safe doesn't open until one. It's on a timer. I told the thieves that. But they didn't care. They just took whatever we had at the moment."

"Okay. Whenever it opens, lock the video in it. I'll be back." Gonzalo turned to go out.

"What about Benji?" Raul asked.

"Cover him with a sheet or something. The ambulance will be here in a little while. Don't let any more customers in. You're closed for the day." He walked out.

Outside there was a small crowd forming. A boy, maybe eight years old, was stooping to pick up a spent cartridge from the gutter near the squad car.

"Hey!" Gonzalo yelled. "Put that down! It's evidence!"

"You got more!" the kid yelled back.

"I said put it down!" Gonzalo made a move toward the boy, who tossed a handful of cartridges back into the gutter and ran away.

"Nobody touches anything!" he yelled out to the crowd. "Everything here is evidence! Don't get your fingerprints on anything!"

An elderly man was stooping to take a closer look at one of the AK-47's.

"Get away from that!" Gonzalo shouted. As many people as had run away from the scene a few minutes earlier now wanted to examine every detail of the crimes that had been committed.

The low horn of an American car was heard being energetically applied, and Gonzalo knew without looking that the mayor of the town was nearing the scene.

Rafael Ramirez was at that time about sixty

years old. He was short and heavyset, with arms that stuck out at his sides and a slight waddle to his walk. Calling him fat would have been something of a mistake. He worked a successful farm on the outskirts of town with his own hands, so his back was powerful and his arms thick with muscle. He was also known to walk some four miles into town on Sundays to go to church, though what effect the church may have had on him was never known by his constituents and must have been completely internal in nature. His brusqueness was famous.

Ramirez jumped out of his car and crossed the street to Gonzalo's side at a near run.

"What the hell happened here?" he demanded.

Gonzalo ignored him. What had happened seemed clear enough.

"Why is Collazo sitting on the sidewalk?"

"He got shot," Gonzalo answered.

"Why is that young cop, the lady, sitting next to the car?"

"She got shot."

"What about the lady cop over there, lying down?"

"She got killed."

"Where's Hector?"

"Chasing the bad guys," Gonzalo said.

"By himself? Where's that other new cop, the man?"

"Fired."

"You picked a fine time to fire people," Ramirez said, just barely crossing his arms across his chest.

Gonzalo ignored him. He had an obligation to report to the mayor, but he was in no mood for Ramirez's coarse questioning.

"Look. I need you to secure this scene. Make sure no one takes a gun or a bullet. I've got to find Hector. I've got to see where the ambulances are. Can you get someone to drive my deputies to the clinic or into Ponce? They need help."

"You're shot too."

"Just do what I say, for once. I'm too busy to be shot."

Gonzalo jogged off to the station house to call Mari quickly. He pulled open the station house door. The air inside was dank and heavy with the smell of drying cement. He made the call standing at his desk, not too worried for his wife's safety. If Ochoa had ever held any thoughts of threatening Gonzalo's family, he certainly had to be giving it a second thought now that the Angustias police force had dropped five of his men to the ground.

"Did you call Molina?" he asked.

"He said he would be here in ten minutes. That sheriff from Naranjito called. She said she would send a squad car to the house in about thirty minutes."

"Good. You'll be safe. Look. I've got a lot of things to do here. There are a lot of hurt people, and Hector's chasing the bad guys. I may not be home for a couple of hours, okay?"

"I understand."

"I tell you, this is a royal mess."

"Who . . . I mean . . . which officer . . ."

"Rosa Almodovar died. Shot in the head. It was instant."

"Oh my God."

"I watched it happen."

"I'm sorry."

"So am I. Anyway. Collazo and Calderon are both hit, not too serious. I'm trying to get someone to take them to the hospital."

"I'll let you go. Just be careful."

"Uh-huh. Bye."

Gonzalo called the clinic to prepare them for the wounded he had seen walking from the scene. Then he called the several hospitals in Ponce to make sure the ambulances were on the way—ambulances sometimes got lost on their way to Angustias.

Gonzalo's next concern was for Hector. He knew Hector was able to take care of himself under normal circumstances, but this day had not been normal. He wished he had some way of contacting Hector, of keeping track of where the young man was.

As it happened, Hector's pursuit of Sergeant Ochoa was not a very long one. He had never ridden a motorcycle before, but imagined it could not be too different from riding a bicycle. The first minute or so was spent falling far behind the thieves as he experimented with clutch and brake. By the time he was ready to make a serious pursuit, the car was heading into the mountainous terrain that made up most of Angustias.

Once in the hills, at speeds surpassing sixty, then seventy miles an hour, the passenger in the car stuck a shotgun out the window and pulled the trigger. The shot went wide, but Hector recognized the threat and pulled out his own gun.

His first shot clanged against the rear fender. He was aiming for a rear tire. But it was hard work navigating the motorcycle and shooting while racing uphill. His second shot hit the asphalt. He tried to remember how many shots he had left as they made a sharp turn uphill then began to go downhill.

His third shot hit the left brake light. The passenger fired on him again. This time the shot was close, and Hector was certain he heard buckshot whiz by his ear. It was uncomfortable. As he made up his mind to shoot at the riders instead of the car, the passenger stuck his torso out the window. Hector tried to take careful aim at the shooter, but he was too late in pulling the trigger. With a shotgun blast his front wheel was blown out, which at seventy-five miles per hour on a motorcycle had the same effect as running into a brick wall. The motorcycle flew into the air end over end, landing in the underbrush at the side of the road. Hector, being lighter, flew further, stopping only when a five-foot-wide mango tree made him.

He was awake for a moment after landing on the ground at the foot of the tree. The world looked funny from the level of an anthill.

A hilltop farmer who had stopped in his field to watch the high-speed chase saw Hector go down. He threw down his machete and went to his truck. He rushed a bit but imagined Hector was most likely dead. When he went down to where Hector had landed, the young man was unconscious and would not respond even to a hard slap to the face. Still, he was breathing, so the farmer took Hector by the hands and dragged him to the side of the road then lay him down in the back of his pickup.

At the clinic, Dr. Perez X-rayed Hector from head to toe. There was a torn ligament in his right knee and a stress fracture in his right foot, probably caused by inertial forces when the tree stopped him. He had also broken four ribs and had a hairline fracture of his jawbone on the right side. He was severely concussed and whenever he awoke, it would be suggested to him that he stay in bed a few days to let the healing process begin.

Chapter Twelve

The first news Gonzalo received that Hector had failed in his mission to stop Ochoa from getting away came while he was still in the precinct. He had found the first-aid kit and had disinfected his wounds by pouring half a bottle of rubbing alcohol on them. It did not sting nearly as much as he expected. The phone rang while he was trying to wrap a roll of gauze around the wound in his upper arm.

"This is Sheriff Gonzalo."

"You better come out here, Gonzalo."

He recognized the voice as that of Raul Ruiz, the owner of a grocery store in the hills of Angustias that served also as a pool hall, with two tables and a bar where men could have whiskey poured into a plastic cup for a quarter for each half-inch. He usually called when a drunken fight got out of hand. It was early for that, but there had been one rainy night when he called from under his counter as bad men shot up his store. Gonzalo had responded to that call himself, but not before Ruiz had lost a hand to a sadistic thief with a shotgun.

"What's the matter, Raul? I've got big problems here."

"Yeah, well I got a big problem here. Someone just stole a car out front—"

"That's going to have to wait a bit."

"You haven't heard everything. When we heard Chuito's car turn on—you know he has that special muffler on his piece-of-junk car—we went out to see what was going on. The thief left his own car, another piece of junk."

"Tell Chuito he can keep it. Look, I've really got to—"

"There was a body in it, Gonzalo. Sitting in the passenger seat. A young guy, maybe thirty. He has one of those vests on for the bullets."

Gonzalo paused a moment. "Is he dead?"

"He's got a hole in his head the size of a dime. Of course he's dead. Why do you think I'm calling you? I need someone to get this guy out of the parking lot. There are flies already. You know what this does for business?"

"I'll be right over," Gonzalo said. "Don't let anyone touch the car. It might have a bomb in it."

The lie about the bomb was the only story he was sure would keep people from searching the scene. There is a morbid fascination with violence and death that makes it impossible for little children to keep their hands off guns. This same fascination often leads adults to disturb crime scenes, unless they are kept away.

Before leaving the station house for Colmado Ruiz, Gonzalo put out an All Points Bulletin for Chuito's car, but he knew that if Ochoa was smart, he would dump the car soon, opting for one with a more normal exhaust. Chuito thought of himself as a speed demon, though his car couldn't go above eighty unless it were in the cargo hold of a plane. Still, he had put racing stripes along the dented and rusted body of the car, and he had mag wheels with shiny chrome five-point rims. He also had an attachment on his muffler that mimicked the machine-gun sound of some funny car racers.

Gonzalo got into his car and drove to the store navigating the hilly roads slowly, looking to each side to see traces of Hector's motorcycle. Ruiz hadn't mentioned the young deputy. That meant Hector had either lost him and was still looking or had been knocked off the road at some point. Gonzalo drove past Hector's crash site without seeing anything of the motorcycle. The underbrush was so thick that only a much more careful examination would reveal where the machine lay.

Ruiz and Chuito were waiting for Gonzalo as he pulled his car into the parking area in front of the store. They were careful to stand as far from Ochoa's car as they could without moving out onto the road. Gonzalo waved them to his car.

"There's no bomb," he told them. "I just can't risk having you guys leave your fingerprints on the car."

"Why didn't you say so?" Ruiz asked, offended.

"Because this is too important to have you guys on the honor system."

Gonzalo got out and walked over to Ochoa's car. Ochoa's accomplice was sitting peacefully in the passenger seat, his head leaning against the headrest, his eyes open, but focused on no particular thing. Gonzalo ducked his head in through the passenger-side window to make a preliminary inspection.

On the passenger's left side, there was a bag. Gonzalo peeked in and found what he estimated was probably all of the bank's forty-two thousand dollars. A trickle of blood had made its way down the accomplice's neck from a point above the hairline behind his left ear. There was no exit wound.

"Don't let anyone touch the car," Gonzalo told Ruiz.

He walked back to his own car, copied down

174

the license plate number of the getaway car and drove back to town.

Sergeant Ochoa had already left Chuito's car in a ditch and had made a phone call from a pay phone at a gas station in Naranjito. The call had been answered at another pay phone in a gas station in Comerio, and the second part of Ochoa's plan was put in motion. For Ochoa himself, there was little to do but walk brazenly into a diner in Naranjito and have a hearty lunch. There was often no better place to hide than in plain sight.

He hadn't expected to leave his getaway car, but then he hadn't expected to have nearly as much trouble with the police in Angustias. He had seen the squad car in front of the bank and he had waited for Hector to walk away and get safely around the corner before beginning a simple bank robbery that should have taken no more than a minute, perhaps two at the most.

Had he planned on a pimple-faced guard who thought twice about lying on his belly and decided to play the hero instead? Had he planned on a jittery accomplice seeing no better way to deal with this unarmed guard than to blast a hole through him, a blast that alerted a woman cop to trouble? A woman cop who, according to the most recent records, didn't work for Angustias.

He sat down and ordered a full lunch complete with dessert to make up for a missed breakfast and thought of these things. The number of things that had gone wrong was staggering. First, a sheriff from the heart of the island, sixty-five miles from his jurisdiction, had met him on the beach. Then a photographer, known to freelance for the press, had taken his picture. Then men he had chosen himself botched a bank robbery in a hick town, turning what was meant as a diversion into a disaster. A relentless pursuit by a young deputy with too much adrenaline in his veins forced him to ditch his getaway car. He thought he had lucked out with a racing car that could get him far fast. Instead, the car made a terrible noise and barely pushed sixty miles an hour.

Still, if the men in the second car, his reserves, could execute their part of the plan and leave their message clearly and quickly, there might be a chance to save everything. Gonzalo would back off his investigation and remain quiet, that was the main thing.

The bank robbery could be attributed to the bodies left behind. Without video nothing tied him directly to that scene. He hadn't fired a single shot. He had killed his accomplice in the car with the man's own gun. There was nothing concrete to tie him to any actual crime. Even if the photographer somehow escaped the men looking for her

as he ate (a possibility so remote, it hardly mer-
ited thought), her pictures hinted at no more than
the improper handling of a corpse. He thought
this all over very carefully as he waited for lunch.
At worst, he was due for a slap on the wrist from
his superiors—the same superiors who had ordered all he had done.

The waitress brought his food and looked at
him strangely. He stared at her as he swallowed
his first mouthful of French fries. She returned his
stare with a wan smile. "What was she looking
at?" he wondered. As he raised his fork to his
mouth again, he saw what had her attention.
Since entering the bank, he had not taken off his
leather gloves. He swallowed his food, drank
down most of his soda, put twenty dollars on the
table and walked out, cursing his stupidity.

Outside, he shoved the gloves into his pockets,
and when he had turned the corner and saw he
was alone, he slapped his forehead with his palm
three times and muttered "Stupid, stupid, stupid!" He ran his fingers through his hair and
found the rolled-up wool cap he was supposed to
have pulled down around his head once inside
the bank; the wool cap he had not paid attention
to in the bank because so many things went
wrong so fast. He began to wonder if everything
in the world would go against him that day. He
began to wonder then who was out to get him. He

began to wonder how long he could stay in that small town before the authorities heard something over the radio and came looking for him.

Back in Angustias, a car pulled up in front of Gonzalo's home and two men got out and made their way to the front door. Two others stayed behind, smoking cigarettes.

Mari had spent the last twenty-three years as the wife of a police officer, but she was not perfect. When she heard Sheriff Molina's car pull up in front, she very naturally put her handgun on the kitchen counter and went to the door. The men outside were surprised when the door opened in the split second before they kicked it down.

Seeing her mistake, Mari backpedaled, but she had no clear plan in mind for this emergency. The gun was in the kitchen and her daughter was napping in her room. She ran to the bedroom and tried to get in and close the door before the men got to her, but there was a hand on her throat before she could shut the door. She was being pulled out of the room. A tear rolled down her cheek from the sheer pain caused by the grip on her neck. She held the doorknob, snapped the lock and pulled the door closed as she was dragged into the living room. There was no sense in any of this. The door was of the flimsiest kind and the men in her house were big. If they wanted to get into the room with her daughter, they would.

The man with his hand on her throat smiled at her. She put her hands on his arm as though she could choke his arm the way he was choking her neck.

"What do you think we're here for, lady?" he said. All Mari could think of was rape and her daughter. She let go of the man's arm; her grip was having no effect on him anyway. She jabbed at the man's eyes with the fingers of her right hand and in the moment that he blinked and turned his head away from her, she brought her left arm down hard against his choking hand. By jerking back at the same time, she broke his hold.

His accomplice laughed at the scene. The strangler, angry now, took a step towards her, and she kicked into his groin as hard as she could, hitting her target as cleanly as if he had been a mannequin.

The myth, of course, is that such a blow is instantly incapacitating to a man; he'll be left to writhe on the floor for a half-hour. More realistically, a kick to the groin is about as incapacitating as a kick to the jaw. Either one can floor a man of any size; either could also fail. The added advantage to a kick to the groin is that men never fail to be surprised by such an attack and they never fail to overreact in guarding against it. They lower their defenses completely once the attack is perceived. That is what happened in this case. The attacker who was kicked put both hands to the affected area and took two steps away from Mari. A small victory. The other intruder punched her in the right temple, crashing her into the cement wall without a sound.

Mari had always thought that if a large enough man punched her, she would necessarily be knocked unconscious. This is also an exaggeration. Even for the most vicious heavy-weight boxers, the knockout punch is usually one that follows a string of other, very effective punches. She felt dizzy after this first punch, and certainly her arms would do nothing she asked of them, but she was still very much conscious and still on her feet.

The man's second punch landed squarely between Mari's eyes. Her vision became clouded except for the man's face lit with anger. The third punch landed on the left side of her head. She could see that the man she had kicked was now stepping toward her. He kicked her abdomen and she doubled over. As she was about to fall to the ground, he grabbed her by the shoulder and propped her up against the wall, holding her there with his hand on her throat again. With his free hand he punched her jaw once, then again.

She swallowed blood and knew she had bitten her tongue. She waited for another punch, but it didn't come. Instead, her assailant let go of her altogether, and she began to slide down the wall to the floor. From the floor, she looked to her attackers. Sheriff Molina had them both in hand.

Molina had been called at Gonzalo's suggestion because no one he knew was better able to defend against people of a purely violent nature. He had been drafted into the Korean War and had been part of the famous battle to take Hill 391. The three days of intense hand-to-hand combat were the best three days of his life. Only in violence was he truly comfortable. He used to chide Gonzalo, "Would God have made me like this if he didn't want me fighting?" And he had a point.

Molina had the muscular neck of a baby bull and fists that looked like they were holding a roll of quarters. He was nearing sixty then, but only a few weeks earlier he had come up behind a barroom troublemaker and pinned his head to the counter while calmly ordering and drinking a shot of rum. The man struggled until he got sleepy and collapsed when Molina released him. This man, who loved violence and had the physique for it, was Mari's savior at that moment.

He grabbed both men from behind and threw one of them away like a rag doll. The other man slipped away from him and turned to face him, his hands up like a boxer's. Molina squared off against him but the man he had thrown aside quickly recovered and put him in a full nelson. The man posing as a boxer in front of him made free to punch Molina once, then again in the gut right under the ribs. This made him mad.

Molina locked his right foot behind the knee of the man holding him and kicked out with all his strength. The two fell, the sheriff of Comerio on top of his assailant. On the floor, Molina knocked his head backward into the other man's nose; when the man still wouldn't let go, Molina quickly dribbled his head back several more times. The grasp on him loosened and he struggled free with a fierce, low growl. The man who had been holding him was now holding his nose.

On his feet again, Molina rushed the man who had given him the punches to the abdomen. The man swung for Molina's head, and in one quick move Molina grabbed the fist, gave it a sharp twist, and knelt, bringing the man's arm down onto his knee. Mari remembers the sound of the man's elbow popping backwards so distinctly, it makes her nauseous to think of it even now.

The man with the broken nose still lay on the floor nursing it with one hand, and when he saw Molina walking towards him, he held up his free hand in surrender. He made some sounds muffled by the blood in his nasal passages. They might have been indications that he was willing, eager even, to have this fight done with and be arrested. Another officer of the law would have been happy to hear this. Molina, however, was a sadist.

He stood beside this attacker and studied him a moment, not knowing where to begin hurting the man. The man moved slightly, and Molina stomped down into his ribs with the heel of his right shoe. The attacker with the broken arm made a motion to hobble by Molina to the door, carrying his right arm in his left hand like a precious and fragile vase. Seeing him out of the corner of his eye, Molina kicked out with the steel toe of this same shoe. The man fell face first to the ground, motionless. A half dozen of his teeth were sprayed onto the floor next to him, but he would not need them again.

Molina walked up to the body and announced that he was going to check the man's pulse. The man's face was turned away from Mari and Molina knelt by his head, blocking Mari's view of what happened next. She says—in private, to those she trusts, and even then with the caveat that she can't be positive of what she believes on this point—she says Molina put a hand on the man's shoulder and one hand to his chin or neck. Then he leaned in close to the man's ear and whispered something. Then he yanked on the man's chin and snapped his neck.

Molina claims the neck was broken by the kick, and that he only touched the man's neck to find a pulse. He didn't whisper anything into the man's ear, he says. He only leaned close to check for breathing.

Molina next moved to the man with the broken nose.

"Molina," Mari called to him. Her head was clear now, but her body was still listless.

Molina looked at Mari, and then quickly knelt next to the man, who was now crying with pain.

"Tell me where it hurts, you little son of a bitch," Molina growled, and he grabbed into the man's chest where he had already broken a rib and began to knead the flesh. The man cried out with a sound that could have come from any dog, and Molina laughed. Then he moved on to help Mari get to her feet.

Like many men for whom violence is a way of life, Molina was capable of feeling great compassion for the victims of violence. Mari was truly a pitiable sight, and Molina was brought almost to tears seeing her.

"My God, those bastards really did a job on you. You're bleeding." He fished a handkerchief from his back pocket. His exertions had not made him sweat or even breathe hard.

"How's that guy?" Mari asked, pointing at the now toothless attacker.

"Him? Dead. The other guy's still alive," Molina answered.

The other guy was writhing on the floor, gasping for air, and spilling blood from his mouth. Mari was as agitated as Molina was unconcerned.

"He could die."

Molina looked at her, astonished that she would care to think of such a thing.

"So?" he asked, and he meant it.

Molina helped Mari sit on the sofa.

"Shouldn't we call an ambulance?" Mari asked. She was still holding her abdomen from the kick she had received.

"If you really feel bad, I can drive you myself."

"Not for me, for him." She pointed.

"Believe me, he's not worth the gasoline that would be wasted on him. Nobody would miss him if his worthless life ended right now. Isn't that right, you piece of shit?" Molina kicked the man's leg.

"Molina. He has a mother."

Molina laughed. "This *hijo de la Gran Puta*? I doubt he could pick out the whore who had him or his pimp father—"

"Molina."

"All right, all right. Give me a second to secure the area in case any of their friends are hiding in the bushes, okay? Look, here's my mace spray. If he moves a hair, squirt him in the face like this." Molina sprayed a stream of mace into the man's face.

"I got it. I got it," Mari said, and she took the mace from Molina.

The only closed door in the house was the one leading to little Sonia's bedroom. Molina opened this door with a kitchen knife, after asking whether the gun on the counter was Gonzalo's.

"These only work if you keep them in your hand," he said, coming out of the kitchen.

"I thought their car was your car. I got careless."

"What car? They don't have a car outside," Molina said, opening the bedroom door.

Sonia was sound asleep. She had inherited her mother's ability to sleep through anything. Molina signaled to Mari that her child was undisturbed and closed the door again.

"There was a car out front. I heard it pull up as clearly as I hear you talking to me," Mari insisted.

"Well, there was nothing there when I got there. Maybe someone drove them over and dropped them off."

"Then they'll be back," Mari said, with horror rising in her voice.

"Not with my squad car out front. Look. The way I understand it, these guys want to scare your husband, right?" Molina asked.

"Oh my God," was Mari's response. She got up from her seat.

"What?"

"Luis's mother. She lives down the road. Left-hand side. They know where she lives." Mari's eyes were opened wide, and she brought her hand to her lips.

"Don't panic. Okay? Panic doesn't help anyone. Here's the phone." He pulled it closer to her. "Call yourself an ambulance. Call my station house; here's my card. Tell them the situation. I'll go over to her house and check it out. It's probably nothing. Just let my men know where I am, okay?"

Mari nodded and began dialing as Molina left the house.

Chapter Thirteen

The sheriff of Naranjito, Susanna Ortiz, was on good terms with every other sheriff on the island and had numerous connections among the Metropolitan Police. Her skin was a healthy cinnamon color, her eyes were a lively light brown, her figure was an array of soft curves, and her smile was warm and made men feel safe in revealing to her the secrets of their souls. She did not need to make an effort to maintain her contacts fresh; officers made their own excuses to talk with her.

In her years as Sheriff of Naranjito (she was only twenty-nine, but had been sheriff for several years already), she had collected numerous promises and accumulated a great number of favors owed her. When Gonzalo asked her assistance in this case, when she heard of all that had happened in front of the bank, she immediately called in a half dozen favors to get the information he needed to carry on his investigation. Her relationship to him was special. Sheriff Ortiz was the first female sheriff in the history of Puerto Rico, and Gonzalo was the only other sheriff who had made her feel welcome. He counseled her in her first year and still acted as her mentor. Though he denied it, she was sure he had spoken to some of the other sheriffs, getting them to stop their constant second-guessing and verbal harassment.

More importantly, at the end of her first year, she had arrested a young mother for the arson murder of her three children. The gross nature of that case had brought her to drink more than was healthy, and Gonzalo was the only one of her peers who had the courage to look her in the eye and tell her she was ruining her life and helping no one. And Gonzalo advised her throughout that brief but difficult period, taking her calls and making time to listen to her fears and frustrations even at three in the morning without a word of reproach. For this she was grateful and swore that she would rise to every occasion Gonzalo needed her help.

When the call came from Mari that there was serious trouble, that it involved the Metropolitan Police, that violence had occurred and more was feared, she hesitated only the smallest fraction of a second before deciding on a course of action.

She would go to Angustias personally, though it was her day off and she was in her street clothes. First, however, she coordinated which officers from her precinct would follow. After rearranging the patrol schedules in Naranjito to make up for the gap in manpower, she clipped her badge and her gun to her waistband and covered them with her sweatshirt. She was tying her hair into a ponytail when another call came for her. It was Gonzalo.

"I desperately need your help," he started.

"I'm coming over, right now."

"No, no. I mean yes, but what I need right now is some information on one of the guys we killed over here. He had an old letter in one of his pockets. It's addressed to an Abelardo Beltran. I think he may have been in prison."

"Sure, I'll put in a call and have them contact you. Why the rush on this guy?"

"I need information, that's all. I can't go to war without it. These guys had *Fuerza Choque* bulletproof vests," Gonzalo said, referring to Puerto Rico's elite riot police group. "But they also had tattoos, the kind you see on prisoners. I want to know which it is."

Sheriff Ortiz put in her call to the Department of Corrections and got through to a clerk who didn't owe her any favors but wanted to very much. He insisted on giving her the information personally (who wanted to get back to Gonzalo?) and put her on hold for only four minutes before telling her what she wanted to know.

"This is a little strange. His record shows he was released early this morning . . ."

"What's so strange about that?" Susana asked.

"I mean *really* early. He was let go at one-thirty in the morning. No parole papers; not much paperwork at all. A lot of blank space where there should be signatures. One name, Sergeant Nestor Ochoa, is typed in. One lieutenant scribbled a signature; there's a mark where the judge's signature is supposed to be. I wouldn't really want to guess who it was. Anyway, does that help?"

"That's excellent. Can you make me a photocopy of what you have?"

"I can't just give these records out. I could lose my job."

"I'd owe you a big favor if you could do it for me."

The clerk's mind raced with the possibilities that big favor might entail in the half second before he agreed to do as Sheriff Ortiz asked.

"Oh, and Michael, I might need you to look up a few more things before the day is over, so be prepared. Okay?"

Few things could have been more okay in the clerk's thinking than earning more favors from the sheriff of Naranjito.

Outside of her own station house, Susana Ortiz walked briskly to her car, which she had left in front of her home near the town plaza. She rounded the first corner in the walk home and saw a man she had never seen before take a cap off his head and then slap his forehead three times, muttering something she could not hear. He then shoved the cap and what looked like gloves into his back pockets. He walked in a tight circle, once, then twice and stopped facing a wall. She decided to approach him as he mumbled to the wall or himself or some unseen friend.

"Do you need help?" she asked.

He turned to her, startled. "Ah . . . No . . . Yes. Can you tell me where the nearest pay phone is? I need to make a call. It's very important."

"Sure. Follow me."

Sheriff Ortiz turned and headed back toward the station house. She had some idea already that if the stranger wasn't the man Gonzalo wanted, he was at least up to no good. Few people in Puerto Rico even own wool caps; she wasn't sure what she had seen was a ski mask, which would have marked him as a thief instantly, but at the very best the cap, along with the agitated movement, marked him as unstable and worth watching.

The station house in Naranjito is part of a larger nondescript government building. The façade at that time was a sand yellow with no markings on the outside to indicate its purpose. If you were not a resident of Naranjito, you could only surmise that the building was for official use from the completely blank stare presented by the exterior.

"What is this building?" Ochoa asked, as Sheriff Ortiz held the door open for him.

"A government building. Look, the pay phone is in the lobby. See it?" She pointed.

Sergeant Ochoa walked in, thanking Officer Ortiz as he went. She followed him in, walking to a water fountain next to the entrance.

As soon as he had finished dialing, she pulled her weapon and walked calmly toward Ochoa, keeping the gun behind her back. An officer came into the lobby from a set of stairs at the far end, and with her eyes she let him know the man on the phone was a suspect to be captured.

Ochoa began talking when Ortiz was only a yard away.

"I'm stuck in Naranjito. I'll stay here for a little while. You have to think of a way to make this all look good. Everything went wrong in Angustias. I mean it. Everything. Look, I can't talk. I have to keep myself out of sight for a little—" He felt his cap being yanked from a back pocket. He turned on Sheriff Ortiz.

"What the hell are you—" he began, but then he was looking down the barrel of her .45. A second gun was quickly shoved into the small of his back.

"Hey, Ochoa. You still there?" the receiver called to him. Then there was a dial tone.

"Who are you?" he asked quietly.

"I'm the sheriff of this town."

"A woman sheriff? Impossible."

"There are two of us now. I was the first. Now put down the phone. That's right, let it hang free, good. Now put your hands up, slowly, good . . ."

"Can I tell you something, sheriff? You and your helper here have managed to set up a cross fire. If either of you pull the trigger, you'll hit me then the other officer. Maybe one of you should change your angle a little."

"Why? Are we going to need to shoot you?" Ortiz asked, and Ochoa looked up to consider the question.

"Yes," he said, and he brought his hand down on the sheriff's hands, pushing them to the side in one move and running for the door. The deputy behind him raised his gun to point to the ceiling. The two officers went out the door a fraction of a second after Ochoa, Sheriff Ortiz yelling at the top of her lungs to gain the attention of her other deputies.

In running his race away from the Naranjito station house, Nestor Ochoa was handicapped by a mistake he had made, one not easily correctable because it had occurred some years before. He had allowed himself to get so out of shape that he was panting as he turned the corner. He had allowed this state of affairs to come to pass because he was making so much money the last few years, he fully intended to retire within a year or two. On the other hand, both the officers behind him were in their twenties still, and Sheriff Ortiz did not tolerate deputies who didn't exercise. Ochoa could hear their footsteps gaining on him. He threw himself into a roll behind a parked car, and pulled a .38 from an ankle holster on his right leg. He took careful aim at the deputy who was trying to target him and pulled the trigger. Sheriff Ortiz saw her man stagger back and sit against the cinder block wall, his hand clutching his chest, but she wasted no time going to his aid. Instead she came to a stop and drew a bead on Ochoa's head.

"Surrender or I'll shoot!" was her order.

Ochoa stood slowly and raised his hands along with the gun above his head. "Okay. You win," he said, then he made a final dash for freedom; the sheriff's bullet hit his left thigh, and he sprawled to the ground. His gun slid a yard away, and he tried to pull himself along the ground to reach it. Ortiz's foot covered the gun just as he was about to put a hand on it.

Ortiz crouched next to him, still standing on the gun.

"You're just a plain old bad man, aren't you?" she asked him.

Ochoa gave a short laugh. "You don't know me," he said, and he turned his face away from her.

"Well, maybe not. But I know two things. First, I know you have the right to remain silent and to have an attorney present during questioning; if you cannot afford an attorney, one will be appointed to you. If at any time you choose to give up your right to remain silent, your words can and will be used against you in a court of law." She yanked his arms behind his back and cuffed them with handcuffs given to her by one of the many officers who were now everywhere on the street.

"What else do you know?" Ochoa sneered.

"I know you hurt one of my deputies, and I will personally make sure you bleed for that." She pulled Ochoa to his feet.

"Think I'm afraid of a girl playing cops and robbers? Go to hell," Ochoa answered.

Ortiz pulled him close to her and whispered in his ear. "Sheriff Gonzalo wants to talk with you. He may even make a deal with you about how you are charged. I doubt it, but maybe. But whatever you are charged with, whatever time you do, you can be sure I will meet you one more time."

Ochoa laughed, but fell silent as he saw the officer he had shot on his feet, talking with other officers, showing them his shaking hands, and taking a glass of soda from a civilian.

"Don't look surprised, Ochoa. Just because we're not *Metropolitanos* doesn't mean we haven't heard of bullet-proof vests. All my officers wear them on duty."

"That's why you didn't stop to help him," Ochoa said.

"No. I didn't stop because you had to be caught. That vest is the reason I shot you in the thigh instead of the head."

She dragged him into the precinct, and after photographs and fingerprints, she pushed him into a cell, his handcuffs back on.

"Hey!" he yelled. "I need medical attention. You can't just lock me in a cell, bleeding."

"Ochoa," Ortiz responded, "you need psychiatric attention, but you're not getting that right now either. The bullet passed clean through muscle; you'll live. Now. Unless you want me to take a look at that wound personally, I suggest you shut up." She turned the key and walked away.

"Cold bitch!" he yelled after her, but she paid no attention.

It was then, when he was alone in his cell, that he began to think of all the people on both sides of the law who wanted him dead, and how few people would care what happened to him. He began to be afraid.

Chapter Fourteen

While Sergeant Ochoa was beginning to worry about his future in a jail cell in Naranjito, Sheriff Molina was creeping his way into the house of Gonzalo's mother. There was a car tucked into the bushes at the side of the house, and Molina knew Sonia Gonzalo had never learned how to drive. As he got closer, he noticed the front door was ajar.

He looked in through a side window and saw Doña Sonia in her dining room, tied to a chair, her arms behind her back, each leg tied to a leg of the chair. Her head was tilted forward as though she were asleep so that Molina could see only the white hair of her head.

A young man, perhaps thirty years old, wearing dungarees and a T-shirt and with shoulder-length hair he looped behind his ears, stood next to the old woman. He was using a steak knife to cut pieces from a half-watermelon. He used the knife to feed chunks into his mouth. He seemed peaceful and paid no attention to his victim. In fact, it appeared to Molina that the man was singing a song in his head because there was slight movement of his hips as he stood there, and he flourished the steak knife like a conductor's baton while he chewed.

From the window, Molina looked around the small house, locating the door he would use to get inside, and plotting a route around the furniture that would put him within a few feet of the criminal without moving through his line of sight. The sheriff of Comerio knew that the element of surprise is the greatest weapon. It consists of a second, perhaps even two seconds, in which you know exactly what you're doing and what you plan to do, but the victim does not.

Molina made his way through the door, through the living room and to the entrance to the dining room. He waited there out of sight, listening to the man hum a tune he didn't recognize. He heard the man call out to another.

"Avanza, Ramón! Tenemos que irnos!" Hurry, Ramón, we have to go.

Molina heard the man slice out another chunk

from the watermelon, then he walked quickly and quietly from his hiding place, crossed the two meters to his target and let loose his fist.

He managed to strike his victim at exactly the moment he wanted. It was the moment when the head was tilted slightly back to receive the steak knife and the speared piece of watermelon. As planned, Molina's fist landed on the man's hand, pushing the steak knife much further into the mouth than it was intended to go. No real damage was done; there was a nasty cut on the inside of the man's cheek and a small nick on the tongue, nothing more. But the man was so frightened by what had nearly happened that he dropped to his knees clutching his mouth shut with one hand and grabbing at his throat with the other, as though Molina had sliced at his jugular. The sheriff landed a right uppercut between the man's eyes that dropped him to the ceramic tile floor without protest.

Molina picked up the steak knife and knelt behind Doña Sonia, cutting through the knots that kept her bound. He heard the toilet flush and saw Ramón come out into the living room.

"*¿Dónde estás, Mañuel?*" Where are you? the boy called out.

He was maybe a little over five feet tall and could not have weighed more than a hundred pounds. He tried later to convince authorities that he was only fifteen so that he might be sent to a juvenile correctional facility, but his age was verified at eighteen. Molina almost pitied him.

The sheriff stood up behind Doña Sonia, and Ramón stared at him with the eyes of a rabbit about to be crushed by a truck—and that is what happened to him. Molina charged at him, putting his shoulder down at the last moment, carrying the stunned boy into the cement wall. All the air was knocked out of Ramón, and he was unconscious when he hit the floor. Molina went back to the task of freeing Doña Sonia. She slumped forward as the binds loosened.

Molina went to the phone in the living room to call for an ambulance and a squad car from his own precinct. Then he went to the watermelon on the dining room table, sat in front of it and cut out a piece with the steak knife and fed it into his mouth.

In Angustias, Gonzalo was at that time in the only clinic in town. The clinic had recently changed its name from the very functional Clínica Medical de Angustias to La Clínica Mendoza. The name change occurred after Martin Mendoza, the richest man in town, with hundreds of acres and several business properties both in and out of Angustias, gave them a donation of nearly two million dollars. This was done, in part, as a solution to a tax problem Mendoza was suffering through, but the clinic's administrators were ecstatic nonetheless. They added an entire wing to the old clinic with two new beds for overnight observations (besides the two they had always had) while increasing the staff from one full-time doctor and one nurse to three of each. The effect on the clinic's clientele was impressive, and that year they would have shown a profit for the first time in their existence if only one more two-dollar aspirin had been ordered.

Iris Calderon was having her leg put into a plaster cast in the examining room nearest the entrance. Dr. Perez, the senior staff member, was working on her. She smiled and waved at Gonzalo as he entered the clinic, then she grimaced as Perez shifted his hold on her leg. Her pant leg was cut off at the knee and there were blood stains on the front of her shirt. Gonzalo made a detour into the room.

"How are you doing?" he asked.

"Fine. I'm okay. I broke my arm when I was ten. This is about the same. In fact, this wasn't even a full break."

"And the bullet?" Gonzalo addressed Dr. Perez.

"It wasn't a bullet," the doctor said without turning from the foot in his hand. "Believe it or not, there was a sharp pebble imbedded in her leg. My guess is it broke off one of the cobblestones when a bullet hit the street. Still, it was big enough and traveling fast enough to crack the bone. I got it out without a problem. There'll be a three-inch scar, and you'll have your deputy back at full strength in six to eight weeks."

The doctor put the last strip of gauze in place and left the room to fetch a pair of crutches and a pamphlet on how to use them.

Gonzalo spoke first. "Has any of this made you rethink your career choice?" he asked.

Officer Calderon pushed herself back on the examining table, letting her back rest against the wall.

"I haven't really given that question much thought yet. I did put down two very bad guys in one day . . ."

"But?"

"But it wasn't anything like training at all. I mean the emotions. I thought I'd feel . . . good about it. Instead, look at my hands." She held them out in front of herself. They trembled slightly but noticeably. "I see those guys. In my head. The first one I got smiled at me before he hit the ground. I never thought I'd kill a smiling man. I . . . I don't know."

"You need rest, Iris. These guys were bad. They would have killed you with a smile and never thought about it again. You did the right thing, and I think you might have saved some lives today. Those guys had heavy weapons on them.

There's no telling what they might have done if you hadn't done your job as well as you did."

"You think so?"

"Trust me. Just getting those AK-47's off the street was a good thing."

"But what about Rosa?" Iris asked.

"Rosa? Rosa didn't make it."

"Oh, I know that part. What I meant was this: Is getting the guns off the street, getting those guys off the street worth Rosa's life? If I had let those guys get out of the bank without resistance, if I had followed them instead of confronting them right there in the street, maybe she'd be alive right now. In fact, if they had gotten away completely, nobody would be injured. I just wonder."

"Forget it. What if's don't help anything. What if those guys had gotten away clean and Rosa lived and they went to another bank and killed twenty people? Would that be better?"

"For Rosa, yes. Don't you feel anything for her? I know you didn't know her too well, and I don't mean any disrespect—I know people handle their emotions differently—but you haven't shed a tear, sir. I mean . . . I mean . . . I mean, what if it had been me?" Officer Calderon shed a tear of her own and her voice became heavy with her emotions.

Gonzalo was silent a moment, having no real answer for his deputy. He had put Rosa out of his mind because there were murderers loose, but he knew her face, lifeless and pasty as he had last seen it, would return to him perhaps even that night in his dreams. She deserved his attention and Gonzalo was sure she would collect what was due her throughout the remainder of his life.

"Don't you feel anything for her?" Iris insisted. Her eyes were filling with tears.

"Don't I feel anything?" Gonzalo echoed. "I will. Believe me. I will. But look at me. I'm not Hector. Hector can outrun criminals. He can outrace them. He can outshoot them. I can't do any of that. If I want to stop a criminal, I have to outthink him. My mind is my only asset. You're right, I didn't know Rosa too well, but she was my deputy, under my command, under my care. I'll cry for her. I would cry for you or Hector or Collazo, too. But first, I have to catch whoever is at the bottom of all this. I have to catch the man who got her killed. Then I can mourn. For right now I need to put my emotions to one side and think with a clear mind."

Gonzalo stopped talking at this point. None of what he said satisfied him. After all, who said he had to stay on the trail of Ochoa? Didn't he know a half dozen nearby and capable sheriffs who would be willing to take over the investigation while he mourned? Was he going after Ochoa for Rosa's sake or for his own?

"I held Rosa's body in my arms," he continued. "I looked into her face, her eyes. I'll remember that until I die."

Gonzalo paused again. The two officers looked at each other, coming to some understanding at that moment.

"Get better, deputy. But stay here until I tell you to go home, okay?"

Calderon nodded, and Gonzalo went on to visit his other officers.

Hector was awake in his bed, propped up by pillows and watching cartoons on TV. He paid no attention to his sheriff.

Dr. Wilma Montez was writing on his chart as Gonzalo walked in the room. Dr. Montez was young and pretty and about the size that made one think she could be fit into a pocket. She was then just out of her residency program, and she was a native of Angustias. Gonzalo remembered her as a child in her yellow and blue grade school uniform. She looked up at him, and he could make out the inch-long scar on her chin, received during a game of kickball with kids who were already bigger than her and with whom she would never catch up.

"How's he doing?" Gonzalo asked. Hector was laughing at something happening to Wyle E. Coyote.

"Officer Pareda will be fine. His ribs have been

wrapped up; his foot is in a cast, his knee will need a little surgery, but that can happen tomorrow. His jaw will heal on its own. He's concussed, so we had him drink some black coffee just to keep him alert. As you can see, caffeine helps him focus on the important things."

"How bad's the concussion?"

"Not bad at all for a concussion. We've taken a look into his head and found nothing. Nothing to worry about that is. We'll just keep him overnight to be sure."

"Well, it looks like you're taking great care of my deputy. Thanks a lot. I really need him back on his feet as soon as possible."

"Oh, please." Dr. Montez smiled and threw a look at Hector over her shoulder. "Trust me, stripping him naked was not a chore. I only wish he was awake when I did it. Maybe next time." She hooked Hector's chart to the end of his bed and left the room, leaving Gonzalo to raise his eyebrows as he followed her out.

"Hey, Boss," Hector started. "Can you believe that doctor? She thinks just because I like the Road Runner, I can't hear what she's saying."

"Relax, Hector. Believe me, there will come a time when women don't look at you anymore. Then you can remember today. Anyway, how do you feel?"

"I'm okay. I can't laugh too loud because of my

ribs. I didn't know they ran cartoons at this hour. I mean the good ones: Warner Brothers, Hanna-Barbera. I've seen what some of the kids like to watch. Terrible."

"Hector, can you concentrate on the chase, before you crashed?"

"Not much to say about that. I didn't get the plate."

"We have the car. Ochoa killed his partner and dumped the car in front of Colmado Ruiz. I'm just fishing here. Did he say or do anything that would give you a clue where he was headed?"

Hector thought a moment, staring at the TV screen.

"Sorry, Chief. Nothing like that. I was just trying to stay on the bike."

"It's all right. I didn't think I'd get anything, but I had to ask. You know how it is."

But Hector was already laughing at something on the television. Gonzalo walked out of the room.

Collazo had his bed at half-recline, and his wife of nearly sixty years, Cristina, was sitting at his side. Whatever their conversation was before Gonzalo entered the room, it ended. Cristina pursed her lips and glared at Gonzalo as he walked in, and he knew that at least one person did not welcome his visit. He knew it was best not to take notice of the anger on her face. She had always seen police work as a young man's profession, and Gonzalo knew she resented the time her husband spent away from home. He often worked the night shift, and she often slept alone.

"How are you?" Gonzalo started, and it struck him at that moment that it was a curious question to ask people lying in hospital beds.

Cristina *humph*ed and turned to face away from the sheriff.

"I'll live. They let me out in the morning."

"Did you ask them when you can return to work?"

"Nope."

Cristina reached for a plastic bag that sat on the floor between her feet. She held it up for Gonzalo to take from her hand. He took it and peered in. Inside were Collazo's badge and gunbelt.

"What's this?" Gonzalo asked, though he had no illusions as to what the gesture meant.

"I can't do it anymore, son. I'm sorry."

Gonzalo wanted to say something to convince his deputy that he could and should continue on the job, but he thought better of it. He stood silent, hoping to force Collazo to fill the noiseless void, but Collazo was comfortable with silence and could not be made to speak that way.

"Can I talk to you later about this?" Gonzalo asked in a low voice, knowing already that he had no cards to play, nothing to offer as enticement.

"You can talk," Collazo said, then he picked up the remote and turned on the TV, and Gonzalo knew it was time for him to go and that anything he had to say later would be in the form of an acceptance of Collazo's resignation.

Dr. Perez approached Gonzalo outside of Collazo's room and handed him a folded piece of paper. They walked toward the front of the building together.

"You had a phone call just now; I wrote down exactly what they told me. Also, your wife is here."

The sheriff shoved the paper into his shirt pocket. "Mari? What's she doing here?" Gonzalo asked, more than a little annoyed.

"Well, I don't know the details. Sheriff Molina brought her in."

"What are you saying?"

"She's suffered multiple contusions to the head. A cut lip, we'll take her for X-rays, but I thought—"

At that point, Gonzalo saw his daughter sitting on a plastic chair in the hallway near the half-open door of one of the examination rooms. On the examining table inside, he caught a glimpse of a hand he knew to be Mari's. He walked in and found his wife.

In the years since that moment, Gonzalo has tried, without success, to separate out all the different emotions he felt on seeing Mari in the examining room. In the first few seconds, he felt dizzy and nothing came to mind for him to say. The one clear thought was "I'll kill him." But besides that there was a jumble of feelings. That he felt like holding Mari in his arms is evident from the fact that he did just that. She cried into his sleeve, and he could feel the slight uncontrollable tremors that passed through her. He thought to himself that it had been several days since he had held a woman who wasn't dead or injured, and he wondered whether he had been afflicted with a form of reverse Midas touch.

"I'm sorry," Gonzalo whispered. "I could have left all of this alone."

"What kind of sheriff leaves a murder investigation alone?" Mari answered. Then, because she knew her husband, she said, "Molina killed the man who did this."

"Good for him. I'll have to get him a keg of beer for his next barbecue." Then, "Let me look at you."

He took her face gently into his hands and examined her closely. There were black rings under both eyes, and a welt forming on her jawline. Half of her lower lip had grown fat and purple. He could tell that her left eye would be swollen shut by nightfall. He touched her chin to signal that she should open her mouth. Her tongue had a small, bright red knot in it, sign of a nasty bite.

Her teeth were intact, however, and he thanked God for that. Though she would have denied it vehemently, she was more than a little vain of her perfect smile, and there was no reason why she couldn't have that back once the swelling in her face subsided.

Gonzalo stepped back and smiled. "I'll get the people responsible for all of this. I think that by the time the day is over, there are going to be a lot of people who will wish they never heard of Angustias. I'm not going to sleep until I find out a few more answers."

"But what about your mother, Luis?"

"Sonia can stay in her house until—"

"Your mother's in the hospital. I think she's in one in Ponce. Perez might know for sure."

"What happened to her?" Gonzalo demanded. He had thought it impossible for the day to get any worse.

"I'm not sure. I think it was a heart attack. Molina found her tied up in her house. He called the ambulance and went with her."

This information had the effect of making Gonzalo hate Sergeant Ochoa even more. He thought to himself, "When I find him, I will make him beg for his life, then I will kill him like a dog."

This was, of course, more fantasy than reality. He had never killed a man in cold blood, and he knew he wouldn't be able to do it now. It is a different sort of man altogether who could dispose of a human life, no matter how vile, without concern for what God thought of the matter. Still, he sincerely wished Sheriff Molina would catch Ochoa. Molina was just the sort of man needed.

With a few more words of tenderness and regret, Gonzalo left his wife in the hands of Dr. Perez. He asked Perez also to find which hospital his mother had been taken to. He was sure it would be disturbing to both Molina and his mother if they had to spend too much time alone together.

Out in the hallway, he sat in a plastic chair beside his daughter and took her hand. They sat silently, and both of them felt that in every way they could imagine, the day had defeated them. Then Gonzalo took out the slip of paper Dr. Perez had given him. It read:

"Ochoa's in custody here. Yours if you want him. Ortiz."

Chapter Fifteen

The shootout at the bank had occurred at a few minutes before noon. When Gonzalo walked out of the clinic to his car, he was surprised to find it was not yet two in the afternoon. He would have guessed that it was late in the afternoon, perhaps four o'clock. It amazed him he had spent so little time on the phone, and in seeing the wounded of Angustias onto ambulances that came into the town at a leisurely pace because the drivers had never heard of Angustias and were unconvinced by the signs that welcomed them.

He felt he had spent a great deal of time waiting to hear that the car left in front of Colmado Ruiz was stolen early that same morning in the city of Santurce near San Juan. He had spent time trying to find where the AK-47's might have originated.

More time was spent viewing and reviewing the surveillance video from the bank. Ochoa's face was clearly seen, as was Benji Carreras's mad, unarmed rush at one of the bank thieves. The thief, much heavier, much stronger than Benji, who was just beginning to fill out a thin frame of bone, pushed him back using his shotgun across the boy's chest. With the young guard a yard or two away, the thief had a choice: he could knock Benji down with the butt of his gun, or he could shoot him. Benji was standing at the very edge of the camera's field of vision; the only parts visible in the split second before the shot were his hands. They went up as though to push some invisible thing in the air. Gonzalo thought maybe the boy had realized his foolishness and was trying to placate the gunman. The shot was fired; the hands disappeared from the screen. Gonzalo estimated that the blast had thrown the boy back a half dozen feet.

He had spent what seemed like hours doing all the police work that would have gone into any investigation. In the end, the break came because Sergeant Ochoa had gotten hungry and careless at the same time.

Gonzalo started up his car, and a strange thought came to mind. He wondered where his only healthy deputy, Abel Fernandez, was. Not that he didn't consider him fired already, but he could have used the help even if it were only for the day.

On the road to Naranjito he passed a TV news van traveling toward Angustias. On another day, this would have alarmed him. He was the only person with any information about the case at all. But he didn't care today. He felt heartsick that his loved ones had suffered. Besides, Mayor Ramirez was a capable man though gruff, and while he had no real information to dispense, he would avoid spreading misinformation.

Gonzalo drove to Naranjito without rushing, taking in the landscape views of the panoramic highway. On a hill far away, probably in the town of Aibonito, he could make out a solitary man in work clothes, wearing a straw hat. The man worked with a machete at clearing away the tall grass, which on the fertile land of a tropical country grew back almost before he had time to turn around. Gonzalo had watched this man many times before, working the same hill, sometimes planting, sometimes harvesting, but usually cutting away at the underbrush. There was no fighting nature, Gonzalo would whisper to the man. Still the man fought, paying no attention.

In Naranjito, Gonzalo found Sheriff Ortiz outside of her station house. She was overseeing the collection of evidence in the shooting of her deputy.

"What happened here?" Gonzalo asked while getting out of his car.

"That *sin vergüenza* shot one of my deputies," Ortiz answered, coming over to greet him.

"Is your man going to be all right?" Gonzalo asked. For a moment he felt that the investigation he had started might wind up hurting people all over the island.

"He'll be fine; he had a vest on. I sent him home for the next three days. His right hand wouldn't stop twitching. I got Ochoa in the leg. Should have blown his head off, the bastard."

Gonzalo smiled to hear her. She was impetuous, like his own Deputy Pareda, but with stronger emotions. He had often thought they would make a handsome couple, but Hector had never tried to gain her attention and had never really gotten it. He had probably shied away from her higher rank and her open expression of every powerful feeling.

They entered the municipal building.

"Has he asked for a lawyer yet?" Gonzalo asked. Dealing with even the most savvy criminals, even policemen who happened to become suspects, was better done without the presence of a lawyer. The accused were often ready to bargain if the evidence against them was strong or thought to be so. Lawyers procrastinated. Worse still, lawyers worked hardest when the suspect was most clearly guilty.

"He hasn't asked for anything yet. I put him in the interrogation room after I phoned you. I figured I'd let him wait a little."

"But you said he has a bullet in his leg?"

"It went clean through muscle. The exit wound was just a flap of skin. He'll live."

Sheriff Ortiz opened the door of the interrogation room and stepped in to make way for Gonzalo.

"There's a recorder there and there should be a few pads of paper in that cabinet. Here's a pen."

Ortiz handed Gonzalo a pen, though he was actually already carrying one, then she left the room, closing the door as she went.

Sergeant Ochoa had taken a seat at the end of the only table in the room. His hands were still cuffed. There were a few other chairs around the table and lined in a row along the wall nearest the door. The cabinet Ortiz had pointed out was small and made of beige-painted metal. It was perhaps three feet high and had a coffee maker sitting on top, but without the glass pot or any of the substances needed to produce an actual cup of coffee.

Gonzalo took a seat near Ochoa, close enough to touch him, and he stared at the sergeant a moment, the sergeant returning his look.

"What?" Ochoa demanded.

Gonzalo shrugged and continued looking, studying Ochoa's face.

"You think you can stare me into telling you something?" Ochoa asked.

Gonzalo shrugged again and sat back in his chair, looking away and smiling slightly to himself.

After a minute more of silence, Ochoa started again.

"Look. This hick-town Columbo bullshit may be fun for you, but my leg is starting to cramp up. I want a lawyer and a trip to the hospital. If you have anything to ask me, just turn on the tape recorder and see what answers you get from me."

Gonzalo looked at the tape recorder as though he were noticing it for the first time. He walked over to it and popped it open, taking out the tape. Then he sat back down next to Ochoa, leaning in closely and speaking softly but clearly.

"I'm not interested in taping you, Sergeant. I don't need your words on tape. I have enough tape of you already. You think that because Angustias is a 'hick' town, the bank didn't have a surveillance camera. I'll bet you didn't even study the bank before you went into it; probably had to ask for directions when you got into town. What was that robbery supposed to be? Some kind of diversion? Did you want me to forget what I saw on the beach in Rincón? Why? What was so important about what I saw there? Tell me."

Gonzalo paused, giving Ochoa an opportunity

to explain himself that he knew Ochoa would not make use of. He was not disappointed.

"If this is your idea of an interrogation, Sheriff Gonzalez, you need to take a refresher course at the academy. Take me to a hospital."

"I'm not trying to interrogate you, Sergeant. I'm trying to talk to you the way one man talks to another. Let me present you with a scenario; you see if I'm wrong. Forgetting all that happened in Rincón, forgetting all that happened in Angustias, don't you think you'll be spending serious time in jail for shooting a police officer here in Naranjito?"

Ochoa rolled his eyes and looked away, saying, "This is useless."

"Okay," Gonzalo went on. "Let me present you with another scenario. Don't respond. You covered up the murder of that guy on the beach because you killed him. Obviously, to do that, you had to be on the boat with him; I'm assuming you didn't catch him in the water and hammer his head in there. But why would you kill a Dominican trying to get to Puerto Rico? Maybe you don't like Dominicans. Still, how would you be able to get other officers to help you? How would you get the *Metropolitanos* from Mayagüez to stay away so you could control the scene? By all rights, it should have been their case to handle.

"I have it from reliable sources that you've been

on similar scenes in Rincón. That's very strange. It's seventy miles away from your station. How could you arrange that? I have an answer: I think you had help. Probably a captain, maybe a commander. Who knows? Maybe a deputy chief or the chief himself. There's a small network, people with some pull, people who can sign prisoners out of jail at all hours of the morning to help you rob a bank. Bad people."

Gonzalo got up and walked a full circle around the table and Ochoa. The sergeant followed him with his eyes, but this was the only indication that he was worried by and attentive to what Gonzalo was saying. It wasn't much of a sign, but it was a good one.

"Now there's one thing I've learned about bad people in twenty-three years of police work," Gonzalo continued. "Do you know what that is, Sergeant? No. I thought not. You're bad yourself. You sent men to beat my wife. You sent men who put my mother in the hospital. You're so bad, you can't see anything—"

"None of that was supposed to happen," Ochoa interrupted. "They weren't supposed to hurt your wife. I didn't say anything about hurting anyone." He seemed truly nervous and was blabbing in a way no lawyer would have allowed.

"But it did happen, Sergeant. That's what I'm trying to tell you. A little philosophy about bad people. Something to think about in prison. Look: You're so bad, you can't notice the bad in others; it's like trying to look at something on the tip of your nose—everyone else sees it before you do. Now here's something I see about the bad people you work with. Bad people hate exposure. Look at your own experience, Sergeant. You went to great lengths to cover up a murder. I suppose you were hoping that man would sink. Maybe you were hoping no one would notice his wounds. You obviously weren't expecting my assistance. I don't think you were expecting my persistence either."

Gonzalo sat next to Ochoa again and leaned in close.

"You're in a very bad position, I think. You clearly have no intention of talking about your co-conspirators, and that's very smart of you. I imagine you've been told what the penalties for talking might be. Who knows? Maybe others have started to talk and been silenced. Maybe even by you. Now you're going to jail. No lawyer is going to ride to your rescue. Will the people you work with trust you to go quietly? What if they have a hint that you've been talking to me? Giving me good leads, bargaining for a reduced sentence. Think of it; the trial alone is going to dig up the fact that there is a conspiracy. That's unavoidable now. Frankly, Nestor—can I call you Nestor? Frankly,

I'm afraid for myself and my family. Right now, my only security is to make your friends think I have information; the kind of information that would harm them if they give me reason to use it."

"I'll never give you that. Don't waste your time," Ochoa sneered.

"I didn't say I had to *have* this information. I said I had to make them *think* I had the information."

Gonzalo went to the cabinet and took out a legal pad. He sat down again, this time nearer to the door, and began scribbling something. When he had grown curious enough, Ochoa spoke.

"What are you writing? I'll deny everything," he said.

"If you really want to see what I'm writing, take a look." Gonzalo pushed the pad across to Ochoa.

"This is a list of things to do. Laundry, groceries, visits to the hospital. What is this? This some kind of joke?"

"No, no. This is your confession, signed and everything. Look. I'm writing 'Rincón' in big letters across the top. I'm writing 'Ochoa' across the middle. Over here, in the biggest letters, I'll put . . . let me see . . . 'Commander'. Over here I'll put 'Lieutenant'. See? It's all very clear."

"I don't get it," Ochoa said, and it was clear he really did not get it.

"It's very simple, Nestor. Can I call you Nestor?

Look. In Angustias, right now, there are a dozen TV cameras. We are getting more attention than we got in seventy-two, when the mayor was killed by lightning. That attention is all due to you; thank you very much. When the TV reporters ask me what happened, I'm going to tell them about Rincón—I'll mention your name, I'll mention questioning you. I'll flash the pad for the cameras. I'll show them the audiotape. I'll tell them there's a conspiracy you're helping to uncover. Maybe I'll tell them how you have changed your ways and seen the light and are cutting a deal; you know, fighting the forces of evil. It'll be on all the networks. You'll be famous. The pictures of you on the beach will be in every paper—"

"They'll kill me," Ochoa said, as much to himself as to Gonzalo.

"Yeah."

"You can't do that. You're a decent guy. That would be murder."

"I prefer to think of it as justice, but call it whatever you want. I'll let you in on a secret. There used to be a place in my heart where I cared for people like you; you know, criminals. I wanted reform, not revenge. Right now that place in my heart is hard and cold. Feel proud, Nestor. You did that. I've got no pity for a guy like you."

Gonzalo got up as though to leave.

"I can tell you anything you want to know

about the Dominican problem. Get me into the federal Witness Protection Program. It's a government plot. I don't know how high up it goes. Maybe the governor knows."

Gonzalo stopped at the door and turned back. He made a move to sit in a chair again, but then he saw a smile spread on Ochoa's face, and he felt that by listening he would be making a pact with a cancer.

He stepped close to Ochoa and jabbed a finger into the wound in his leg before the sergeant could do anything to stop him. Ochoa winced and balled his cuffed fists in pain. Gonzalo whispered harshly through clenched teeth.

"Listen to me good, Ochoa. You hurt my family, you killed my officer, and you killed that man on the beach. I really don't care about what you have to offer. I have other sources. You, my friend, are being hung out to dry. You want advice? Don't get a lawyer, get a reporter. Exposure isn't just my weapon; it's the only weapon. Frankly, if you die from exposure, I won't lose sleep."

Gonzalo gave Ochoa's wounded flesh a twist so that the sergeant breathed hard and a string of drool formed.

"You bastard," the sergeant said, in what would have been a full-lunged yell if he could have caught his breath. "You bastard."

"Yeah." Gonzalo shrugged and let the leg go.

Then he walked out of the interrogation room and closed the door on Ochoa. He walked to the front counter to find the sheriff.

"Anything?" Sheriff Ortiz asked.

"I got enough from him. Listen, can I keep this tape?"

"Does it have anything about him shooting my guy?" Ortiz asked.

"No," Gonzalo answered, and he seemed a bit dazed. "I only talked to him about Angustias."

"Then sure. Here. I'll voucher it out to you myself." She walked to her desk and got a pad from the lap drawer.

In the meantime, Gonzalo thought of his course of action. He had rejected information from Ochoa because he felt at the time that the source was tainted morally. If he did what he promised Ochoa he would do, it would be murder, or at least a kind of murder. He felt sure about that. Pretty sure. Still, it was something Ochoa had brought upon himself, but that didn't satisfy—criminals made those kinds of excuses. Still, he wouldn't be the one pulling the trigger—criminals said that, too. He couldn't say all that he had hinted to Ochoa. He convinced himself of that. But then what would he say? The press was going to ask questions and there had to be some answer. You couldn't simply "No comment" your way through the colossal mess Ochoa had created. He would tell the truth of the matter. Or maybe he would tell some of the truth. Or maybe he could dodge the press. Or say everything he had threatened Ochoa with. After all, if Ochoa didn't deserve . . .

"I said, are you all right?" Sheriff Ortiz was talking.

Gonzalo shook his head sharply to clear his mind.

"I'm fine. I'm fine. It's just been a long day. A very long day."

"Here's your voucher."

Gonzalo took it distractedly.

"Are you sure you're all right?" Ortiz insisted.

"I said I was fine."

"I know but . . ."

"But what?"

"You have blood on your hands," Ortiz pointed out.

Chapter Sixteen

Gonzalo drove into Angustias with every intention of keeping quiet for the press. There would be time later, if it proved to be necessary, to implicate Ochoa. For the time being, he would concentrate on more traditional means of investigation. He would identify the other bank thieves and if they were recently released from prison, he would find out why and by whom. He would follow every possible paper trail to its end. If none of this worked, he would expose Ochoa and wait to see which officers and officials flinched.

By the time he got into town, Angustias had undergone a drastic change. The streets were clogged with people who normally ventured to town only rarely. There were vendors selling *jugo de parcha* and *maví*. It was as though a carnival had come to town or the city had come together to celebrate *Las Fiestas Patronales*.

Gonzalo tried to make his way to his office, but had to leave his car a block away because pedestrians ignored his car horn, and he had no intention of turning on the blue emergency light he carried. As he neared the station house, he saw four vans parked out front (actually three vans and one station wagon). There were two camera crews complete with microphones and hair stylists. There was at least one radio crew. There was a print journalist he recognized, and several others he didn't. And there were photographers. It was a photographer who first noticed him nearing the precinct and called out his name, already flashing away.

"Is it true your wife was killed?" was the first question Gonzalo heard. He had intended to get into his office without saying a word, but he had to answer at least that question.

"Not at all true. Who said that? Where did you hear such a thing?"

The reporter who had asked was a short, thin man with a balding head and glasses. He pressed closer to Gonzalo through a crowd of microphones and cameras.

"They took Mrs. Gonzalo to a hospital in Ponce. She had a stroke."

A female reporter stepped in front of this man. She was no more than twenty years old, Gonzalo thought.

"Is it true you have arrested a police officer for all of this trouble?"

"No comment."

"A Sergeant Ochoa from San Juan?" the young lady insisted.

Gonzalo thought quickly about what to say. He couldn't really go on record with an outright lie, and this woman knew an uncomfortable amount of information. He certainly didn't want to appear to the world as knowing less than a reporter who had never even been to his town.

"Sergeant Ochoa is under arrest in Naranjito for charges related to . . . what happened here today."

"What about Rincón?" the lady continued.

Gonzalo was silent a moment.

"Is that audiotape in your hand part of the investigation?" someone yelled out.

"Is it from Naranjito? Did you just come from there? Is it Sergeant Ochoa's confession? Is he cooperating?"

"Yes," Gonzalo said, though he himself could not have identified a specific question he was answering. "Sergeant Nestor Ochoa is giving evidence. He asked to make a deal. He's telling everything about the robbery here, the shootout, about Rincón, about the smuggling of Dominican nationals to Puerto Rico. Everything. Names, dates, everything. Now excuse me. I have work to do."

Gonzalo rushed through the crowd of reporters, which had grown since he began holding court. He locked the door of the station house behind him and threw himself into a chair. He looked around the station house slowly, trying to get his bearings. Trying to understand the implications of the words he had just then spilled out. He took time to notice also that the cement work was nearly done.

"Those boys work fast," he said to himself.

Then he said, "I've killed Ochoa. If he's mixed up in something as big as I think, he'll be lucky to last the night."

Gonzalo fought back a wave of grief and anger at himself. When he thought of himself, he thought he was first and foremost an intelligent man. He solved cases and brought criminals to justice by outthinking them. He was happiest when tripping up a suspect during an interrogation, catching them in a lie or other inconsistency. He liked to think he could not be caught off his guard in the same fashion. He liked to think he could keep calm and cool in any situation and give out only the information he wanted to give out. For the most part he was right. Criminals living in the center of the island knew they didn't want to be questioned by Sheriff Molina of Comerio—his suspects too often ended up in a hospital bed; worse, some went into the interrogation room and were not seen again. That at least was the rumor. Still, they did not necessarily prefer to fall into the hands of Sheriff Gonzalo—he would make their heads hurt without ever touching them. Their most trivial statements would be replayed in a courtroom and ensure their conviction.

But the sheriff of Angustias had proven defenseless against a few reporters who would have been just as happy with blunt denials. He had attended an all-day seminar on how to deal with the press just a few months before. None of the tactics taught to him had come to mind when he needed them. He should have paid more attention.

He got up and rolled open one of the front windows. Most of the media people had moved on. He decided to make a dash for the bank.

"There he is again!" someone shouted, and Gonzalo walked briskly, almost trotted, to avoid the reporters converging on him.

"Sheriff!" a woman behind him shouted. "Sheriff, they say a photographer was helping you in the investigation and now she's dead. Any truth in this?"

The statement stopped Gonzalo in his tracks. He had forgotten entirely that the photographer was in as much danger as he was and less able to defend herself. In fact, he had forgotten the photographer entirely—only the pictures had been important.

"Who said this?" he demanded fiercely.

"It's on the police frequency in Naranjito. Just now," the reporter responded, with more fear of authority than was fashionable for a reporter.

Gonzalo turned away and continued toward the bank slowly. He turned the information over in his mind. Sheriff Ortiz wasn't fully informed about the case. She didn't know about his contact with a photographer. He tried to remember if he had mentioned pictures—they would imply that he was working with a photographer. His mind came up blank on this point. No matter. Maybe Ochoa had decided to tell all to Ortiz. Maybe he mentioned the photographer. Maybe he told Ortiz where the body was.

Gonzalo stopped and turned to face his pursuers.

"How did the photographer die?" he asked.

"Were you working with her?"

"Answer my question, please."

"It's hard to get a clear reading in this area with all the mountains. Also, there's a thunderstorm starting up in the area of Aibonito—"

"You don't have a clue," Gonzalo said, and turned again.

"They said her car was run off the road somewhere in the hills on your border with Naranjito. They say it rolled over and ended up two hundred feet down the hill. They say a retarded man found her and dozens of photos, photos of the beach in Rincón. The cops at the scene were frantic. I don't know any more, Sheriff."

"Thank you."

"Can you give me her name, Sheriff? Tell me her involvement in all of this?"

"Sorry," Gonzalo said and walked away.

"Can you at least say where that hill is?" was shouted after him, but he paid no attention to the question, and the reporters followed him at only a leisurely pace.

In front of the bank, the carnival atmosphere intensified. There were several more news vans there with antennas raised high above the bustle of the street. Three reporters were broadcasting live with a clear view of the tattered squad car. Mayor Ramirez and Deputy Mayor Jorge Nuñez stood shoulder to shoulder—approximately. Nuñez was thin, and a foot taller than the mayor.

Alfredo Santoni, director of the only funeral home in Angustias, was half-sitting on the hood of his hearse with one foot up on the fender. He motioned for Gonzalo to come over.

"I guess business is booming today, huh?" Gonzalo commented.

"Don't joke like that. People think I'm some

sort of vulture. They make comments all the time. They didn't talk that way to my father."

"Sure they did, when he first took over the business. But he didn't pay any attention and the jokes got old fast."

"Well, all right, but I got work to do. Look. There are no more ambulances. They say there's a fire in Fajardo that's wiping out a whole block. Can you let me do my job?"

"What job? What are you talking about?"

"Ramirez won't let me take Benji out of the bank. He says I have to wait for you."

"The boy's still in there?"

"Someone put a handkerchief on his face, but he's still there. Can I go get him? If I have to wait, it's gonna get bad, you see how it is?"

"Yeah, yeah. Sure, come on."

Gonzalo did not normally suffer from migraine headaches, but he would have sworn he was afflicted with one at that moment. The day had been too much for him, and his head felt as though someone had stuck a screwdriver through his skull at a point three inches behind his left ear and was trying to pull it out an inch or two above his right eye.

Inside the bank, Benji Carreras was in the same position he had been in two hours before. The only difference was that his mother was now kneeling at his side, wiping away tears with a handkerchief. She looked up when Gonzalo came close, and he read an indescribable mixture of grief and despair in her face. It was as though she thought the world itself had sought to destroy her, and Gonzalo knew it almost had. Whatever complaints she had of her son (and, after all, he was still a teenager), she felt her loss to be great now and unmitigated. The sheriff wondered if her life would ever be normal again, and he was glad he had killed Sergeant Ochoa. There was a certain cleansing in an eye for an eye, a life for a life. "People should get what they deserve," he told himself, "and Benji did not deserve this."

"Did you catch the man who did this?" Benji's mother asked.

"Yes. We have him," Gonzalo replied.

"Can I see him?" she asked, and she made a motion with a tight fist as though she were using an imaginary screwdriver. Gonzalo understood her anger. He was sure the screwdriver was plunged to the hilt in Ochoa's heart.

"Not right now, Doña Carreras. Maybe tomorrow," Gonzalo answered.

He turned to go and wondered if he had ever called her "Doña" before. She seemed too young for that title of respect, but grief and great pain are due their own respect and circumspection.

Outside, he whispered his briefing to the mayor

and his deputy. It was the first time they had heard the entire story as far as Gonzalo knew it.

"You mean a cop did this?" Ramirez fumed.

"Yes."

"And now he's caught?"

"He's in the Naranjito prison right now. Saw him there twenty minutes ago."

Jorge Nuñez spoke. "And this is connected to what happened in Rincón the other day?"

"Yes. I helped on the beach there, as I've told you before. The cops who relieved me covered up the fact that one of the victims was murdered. When I investigated too much, when I got pictures of what they did, they decided to create a diversion for me. I think this was supposed to be a simple bank robbery. If they had gotten here an hour earlier, there would have been fewer people in the bank. Hector and Officer Calderon would not have been on duty, and I would have been home. If they had come an hour earlier, it would have been a simple robbery. It would have been a diversion. But you see what happened."

"But how could it be a diversion?" Nuñez asked. "The same man on the beach came to the bank. How is that supposed to divert your attention from him?"

"I don't know. He had a ski mask that he never used. Maybe he forgot. Besides, I don't think the idea was to draw attention from him, primarily. I think he has superior officers, maybe even deputy chiefs, who are involved in this."

Ramirez broke in. "*Humph*. Next you'll say maybe the governor is involved in this."

"Maybe. There's more to it than just this sergeant. I'm sure of that."

"Is it too much to ask that the next time you decide to start an investigation this big, the next time you decide to do an investigation that gets one officer killed, puts three others in the hospital, puts a pimple-faced *guardia de palito* in the morgue—"

Ramirez didn't finish his sentence. He knew he was attacking Gonzalo unfairly even as he said the words, but he had not thought Gonzalo would take a swing at him. Even as he tried to raise himself off the sidewalk in front of the bank, he was telling himself that Gonzalo didn't have enough strength to knock him to the ground.

Nuñez held Gonzalo away from the mayor.

"You want my badge?" Gonzalo asked, ripping it from his shirt. "Here! Take it! You want to be sheriff? Go ahead! Have a good time!"

Ramirez was still in no position to speak. The reporters, who all had their cameras trained elsewhere, were rushing to the front of the bank. Nuñez gently pushed and pulled Gonzalo off the sidewalk and into the bank.

"Nobody wants your badge, Gonzalo," he whispered. "You know Ramirez; he's just like that. He doesn't think before he talks. Remember, you've had a bad day, but he's had a bad day too. Those people who died, who got hurt, they are all *Angustiados*, they are all his responsibility."

Nuñez said all this in a calming tone. It was a tone he had used many times before in dealing with people the mayor had upset. In fact, this tone was the main reason he was deputy mayor, and many said they would not be able to vote for Ramirez if Nuñez did not run with him. He hugged the sheriff as a sign of camaraderie, and Gonzalo clung to him for a moment. Then the sheriff pulled away. It was one thing to be hugged by a man during a trying time as a sign of solidarity, but it was another altogether to sob into his chest. Gonzalo wiped his tears as though something were in his eye, and Nuñez looked away, studying the room as though he had never been in a bank before.

"Look. Gonzalo. Just let me know two things. I just need a little information from you, okay? First, I need to know: Is this it? Are there going to be more people shooting up this town?"

"Maybe. I'm not sure. I don't think so. Certainly not while the reporters are here. Whoever is in charge of all this mess, they don't want people to know who they are. They want to avoid any kind of attention. That's why they did this. It just went very wrong."

Gonzalo ran his hand through his hair and wound up rubbing his neck. The day had already been long for him and it would not end soon.

Mayor Ramirez walked in at this point and walked to Gonzalo, his hand extended toward him. They shook hands, and Ramirez slapped Gonzalo on the back with his customary harshness. This action was both a sign that he had forgiven the punch and an apology for the words he had spilled out.

Jorge Nuñez resumed his questioning. "Secondly, I need to know if we have any allies in this mess. You think the police are rotten, tell me who are the good guys."

"Sheriff Molina and his people, Sheriff Ortiz and her people, and . . ." Gonzalo paused, looking to the ceiling for answers. "And no one else for now. The media will keep bullets from flying until they leave; after that, there are no guarantees. We have some evidence, and Ochoa can give us more. As long as we keep the evidence in our possession, the people implicated in it will keep us in their sights. As long as they're not positive about what we have, they won't pull the trigger."

"You hope," Ramirez said.

"I hope," Gonzalo confirmed.

"But people who are afraid they'll be exposed

might risk coming back to gather that evidence and burn it, right?"

"They might."

"Then I don't know what we're waiting for," Ramirez said.

"What do you mean?" Gonzalo asked.

"I mean, let's fight the bastards. If all we have on our side is evidence and the media, then let's put them together, tell the world what we know and let the *Metropolitanos* watch for themselves."

"You mean broadcast what we have to the public?" Nuñez asked.

"Damn right," was the little mayor's reply.

"But," Gonzalo interjected, "that will ruin the investigation. There's a lot more evidence to collect. We need subpoenas; we need warrants. The people we're trying to get may destroy or hide things. The trial—"

"None of that worries me," Ramirez broke in. "*No me importa dos pitos*. The trial. Who cares about the trial? I care about AK-47's. You have an hour to collect whatever evidence you can, then I'm having a press conference and showing everything we have. Hell, I'll tell them we have things whether we do or not, you understand me? We're on the offensive. You with me on this, Gonzalo?"

"Sure, I guess. Do I have a choice?"

"I don't think there is a choice except to sit

around waiting to be killed. Now I'm going out there to tell the reporters that we'll have a statement in an hour. I want you standing behind me next to Jorge. Don't say anything, just stand there and look like a sheriff. Can you do that?"

"Sure."

"Good. Now let's go. Oh, and Gonzalo, put that goddamn badge back on."

Gonzalo put the badge back on a little higher than usual and to the left of the torn spot on his shirt where it was normally pinned. Then the three men went out to face the cameras.

Chapter Seventeen

Mayor Ramirez made his announcement outside the bank in the briefest manner possible.

"We have evidence about the people in the police department who ordered this bank robbery. We'll be presenting it to all of you in one hour."

He had to repeat these exact same words thirty seconds later, since he hadn't waited for the reporters to approach him before beginning to speak. When he had repeated himself, he began to walk away, not waiting for the print journalists to finish their scribbling onto their small notepads.

"So you're sure the *Metropolitanos* are involved?" a reporter called out to him.

Ramirez turned back to the crowd. "Didn't I just say that?" he asked. "Come back in an hour. We'll show you everything you need."

The reporters went back to their various vehicles, wondering aloud why the mayor was offering information that would normally be kept from reporters. Most came to the conclusion that he probably had very little more than the fact that a sergeant had been arrested.

"He probably just wants to keep attention on this little town of his and get his face on the evening news," said the lady from Channel 4 to a radio reporter from WKAQ.

"Are you staying?"

"Of course, I'm staying. It's either this or drive out to Fajardo to cover the fire. They've got a helicopter there. With the way my soundman drives, we'd get lost for sure and probably end up in Cuba."

The reporters spread out across the town. There was some thought to knocking on doors and getting interviews with the local residents, and a few reporters did this half-heartedly, but even they were soon discouraged when they found that most people had hardly observed the shooting at all.

What stuck in the mind of most of the witnesses was how loud the whole thing had been. One of the men who had spent the whole time crouching behind a car and swiping sweat from his forehead with a handkerchief remarked how similar the experience had been to finding Charlie in the bush in Vietnam. When asked where exactly he had served, he looked stunned and said, "Served? I never served. Television." And the reporters lost all interest in him.

In the meanwhile, Gonzalo had a lot of work to do. He knew that he would not be able to get all the evidence he wanted and that he didn't even know yet what evidence would be most useful to him. His first phone call, however, he thought would be the most helpful.

Sheriff Ortiz took the phone in her left hand. Her right hand was bruised from an attempt to show Sergeant Ochoa how tough she was with the back of her hand. At the same time, Ochoa put on a display of how tough he was. Both officers were smarting, though neither would admit it.

"How can I help you?" she asked.

"You have a way with the administration in San Juan. I need them to get some documents to me. I'm making out the paperwork, and I'll be phoning in for some warrants, but I won't be able to collect these things myself for a few hours to come. I need information. I need to know about the dead guys involved in this bank robbery. One of them was a prisoner released early. I suspect the others were as well. I need their paperwork preserved and delivered up to me ASAP.

"I need to know about the AK-47's. I'm guessing some were seized recently and never made it to evidence. I need to know about the cars. One was stolen in Santurce, but we found another one that was left near the bank. I need a history of where it came from. I need to know about the officers who were in Rincón with Ochoa—"

"Whoa, whoa, whoa. I have a few connections, but I'm not almighty."

"I need all of this within the hour. I'm sending you fingerprints, names, a license plate number; everything I have. It's all going through the fax machine. Wait a minute. The machine is not taking the papers."

"Are you putting them in all at the same time?"

"Is that bad?"

"Very. Feed it one at a time."

"Okay. There it goes . . . it's very slow. Is that normal?"

"Yes."

"Okay, the first one is through. Do you have it?"

"You sent a blank page. Which way do you have the paper facing?"

"The wrong way, I guess. Here. There it goes again. This should be better. Now look. Get as much as you can faxed to you. Send an officer to execute warrants; send a couple. Get me as much as you can in an hour."

"Why the rush?"

"Haven't you been watching the news? We're going to give the press everything we have about the *Metropolitanos*. In an hour, we're going to have a news conference and expose everything we know."

There was silence on the line for a moment. Ortiz was trying to work something out in her mind. "You know you'll jeopardize getting convictions," she asked.

"Our priority is to keep Ochoa's handlers from thinking they can silence us with the right number of bullets. They can't silence us if we broadcast what we have first."

Ortiz remained silent for a half-minute before pointing out what Gonzalo had already considered. "You might be killing Ochoa. He's bound to know more than you can uncover anytime soon. They won't get to him while I hold him, but he has to transfer out of here soon. He needs to be arraigned."

"Keep him as long as you can. It's in his best interest. Convince him that a speedy trial process is not what he wants right now."

"Uh, I'll do my best," Ortiz replied. "Anything else?"

"Yeah. One other thing. The photographer; which hill is she on?"

Ortiz gave him the highway marker number, and he thanked her profusely for her help, saying that he owed her. She protested, saying that she was still deep in his debt, but he told her he would keep his own accounts.

"I won't forget your service, Sheriff," he said to her and hung up before she could reply.

There was an irresistible urge within Gonzalo at that hour to visit the body of the photographer, to see her, maybe touch her skin. It seemed a meager tribute to a young woman he had met on a bloody beach and who had gambled and lost everything she had in the universe, betting that he could help her to do good.

The area where the photographer had gone off the road was a neighborhood of Angustias known officially as Barrio La Cola—The Tail. It was on one of the highest hills in Angustias—in fact, one of the highest hills in Puerto Rico—and on the map it was drawn as a long and relatively thin strip of land that ran at an angle to the bulk of Angustias, hence the official name.

Unofficially, the people of Angustias changed two letters and called the neighborhood El Culo—The Ass. While most of the people in Angustias were poor, the six or seven families that were the only residents of the area were charity cases. The children rarely wore shoes before reaching school age and rarely finished even elementary school. Gonzalo had arrested three parents for failing to bring their children to school, but this did nothing to discourage truancy. The people of El Culo were poor and destined by their own actions to stay that way, possibly for generations to come, hence the unofficial name.

The road through La Cola is still made up of patches of broken asphalt interspersed with spots where the ground is covered only with gravel and stretches where the red clay earth is not covered at all. The forest on either side of the road is thick, untouched. There are no streetlights in this area, and the driving is made doubly treacherous by the fact that the road is filled with sharp turns and is only just wide enough for one car to pass, though it is by necessity a two-way street.

When you finally reach the end of the road, you have climbed to a height of a little more than three thousand feet above sea level. It will have taken you something more than six miles of twists and turns to get to the end, and the end is just that. Without warning, without a single sign, the road through La Cola terminates in a foot or two of underbrush. Beyond that there is nothing but an almost-perpendicular drop of several hundred feet. The terrain is covered with tall grasses and choking vines, with a few fruit trees growing uncared for among them.

The only other interesting thing about the end of the road in La Cola is the fact that someone had actually built a house made of cinder blocks and concrete up there. That was why the road extended that far. The new owners found that though they offered to pay for water lines to be constructed, no one would undertake the project at any price. So the man—nobody now remembers his name—and his family lived in their home for weeks, then months, without water and light. Then they left, perhaps a dozen years before this story began, never bothering to try to sell the land that, it was later found, they had never bothered to buy in the first place. The front porch of this house and its driveway was the command center for the effort to retrieve the photographer's body.

When Gonzalo got there, three patrol cars were lined up as close to the cement walls of the house as possible. There were six officers from Naranjito trying to figure out a way of getting to the car. From the tears in one uniform, Gonzalo could tell that the direct approach—simply walking down the steep hill—had been tried.

Gonzalo stepped out of his car and walked toward the huddle of officers.

"How's it going?" he called out.

A young deputy wearing shades spoke up first. "It's not going, sir. That car's about five hundred feet down. Navarro here tried to go down slowly, but this hill had a different idea. He's lucky he didn't break his neck."

"How are you, Navarro?" Gonzalo turned his focus to the man with the torn uniform. He had a small cut and a large welt near his left eye.

"I'll live. I just took three steps, then I slid about fifty feet. Look, you can see how far down the car is."

The group of officers walked to the end of the road and felt their way through the underbrush to a point where they could safely look down the hill, but they could not take another step. The car was turned onto its hood. A clear line of flattened grass and broken saplings showed exactly how the car had skated to its resting place at the side of a mango tree. Much of the vehicle was obscured by vegetation, but the wheels in the air guaranteed that the end of the road had been unkind to this car.

"Any clues of how this happened? Did she just drive off by accident?"

"No, sir. Definitely not. Look. Skid marks here at the edge where the pavement turns to dirt. Over there," the man in shades pointed back onto the road, "we found bits and pieces of headlight glass and grillwork mixed up with some taillight plastic. The car was hit from behind by a car going at a pretty good rate and pushed off the road." The officer made motions in the air with his hands to recreate the scene he was describing.

"So you think there was a chase, and it ended here when the victim stopped because there was no more road and the pursuer caught up."

"I'd say so," sunglass man said.

Gonzalo looked down again at the car. It was certainly much closer than five hundred feet; perhaps half that distance. But Angustias was filled with steep hills, and he knew that cars that were even closer to the road sometimes could not be reached without a helicopter.

"Come on," he said, and the officers followed him to the trunk of his car. He pulled out a hundred feet of yellow nylon cord. "You guys have rope, don't you?"

"Sure. Two of the cars do, but I don't think they'll reach," Navarro said.

One of the other officers went to get the rope, and Gonzalo knotted the three lengths securely together. Navarro began to tie the rope around his own waist.

"What are you doing?" Gonzalo asked.

"I'll go down the hill."

"I think you've had enough of this hill. I'll go down. I've done this before."

"Then I'll anchor you," Navarro said.

"You've got heart, deputy. I like that. Frankly, I'd rather you got one of those squad cars and anchored me to that."

Navarro untied himself reluctantly and went to fetch a car.

"Gather up the headlight glass and grill plastic. I might be able to find out what kind of car we're looking for," Gonzalo said to the officer in sunglasses.

"What about the taillight plastic?"

"What about it?"

"Don't you want any of that?"

"We know which car left that."

"Oh. Right."

The officer in sunglasses whispered to another officer and that officer went to begin the process of bagging crash debris. Sunglass man pulled driving gloves from his back pocket and pulled them on, flexing his hands as though he were getting ready for Indy. When the car eased near, he personally tied the rope to the front fender.

"No, no," Gonzalo said. "Not too many fenders are reliable enough for that. Doesn't the car have a trailer hitch?" Gonzalo stepped to the rear of the car and tied the knot himself. "There. That ought to hold me. Now here, Navarro, take the rest of this rope and toss it as far out as you can. Toss it high."

Navarro did as he was asked, impressing the sheriff with the power of the toss. Gonzalo looked the deputy over. He was only of average height, but very muscular. He wondered how many times in his young career the deputy had been asked to do the things that required brute strength.

Gonzalo let himself down the hillside, half rappelling and half holding on to the rope out of terror. He knew that if he broke his leg in the descent, it might be hours before he was rescued. Just as he was thinking that thought for the tenth time, he slipped on the giant leaf of a Malanga plant that had been matted down by the passing of the car. His knee struck a rock outcrop, and he clenched his eyes shut from pain. After a moment he forced his leg straight so that he knew nothing was broken, but opening his eyes and taking a look he saw he had torn a hole in his pants big enough to pass a grapefruit and that there was more blood there than had come from the wounds to his arm.

"Come on, Gonzalo," he told himself, "this is your problem. Those guys are a hundred feet away and you've got the only rope."

Navarro yelled something to him.

"I'm all right!" Gonzalo yelled back, taking a closer look at his knee. He was sure he was looking at exposed bone.

"No!" Navarro yelled. "We found her! We found the driver!"

Gonzalo looked up from his knee and watched as the photographer moved into place next to Navarro. She waved to him, and Gonzalo waved back and began to climb his way uphill.

Chapter Eighteen

The telephone rang and rang in the station house in Angustias, but there was no one to pick it up. The only able-bodied police officer Angustias had was having trouble climbing up a hill in one of the loneliest regions of central Puerto Rico. In fact, while getting down the hill had been a long and sweaty ordeal, getting back up the hill proved much worse. Gonzalo was still on that hill as the deadline for presenting the evidence approached and, not able to contact him by phone or reach him on the CB, Sheriff Ortiz decided to gather the information she had gotten and drive to Angustias personally.

Mayor Ramirez was slamming the door of the station house as she parked her car in front.

"Who are you?" he barked at her.

"Susanna Ortiz, sheriff of Naranjito," she answered calmly, offering him her hand.

"You know about what happened here?" he asked.

"I know more about what happened here than anybody," she said.

"Good," he answered. "Let's go." He took her hand and didn't let go, dragging her behind him toward the town plaza.

"What do you want from me?" Ortiz asked. She wondered how little effort it would take to dump the little mayor on his ass.

"I need to show the press the evidence we have about the people who did this. Cops, right?"

"Definitely, but I can't do a press conference now. I look like a mess."

Ramirez stopped and turned to her, looking her over from head to toe.

"You'll do," he said and pressed on for the plaza.

The first images through the camera lens were of the diminutive mayor dragging the very tall Sheriff Ortiz behind him. The first question was, "Where is Sheriff Gonzalo?" but Ramirez didn't know the answer to that question so he ignored it. He took his place behind a lectern Jorge Nuñez had placed under a tree near the plaza's fountain.

"I promised you evidence that the *Metropolitanos* were involved in what happened here today.

257

First, I have a name here ... let me see ... Sergeant Nestor Ochoa. He works in El Condado. He was here shooting at people. Now he's in jail in Naranjito. Next, I got photocopies of pictures of something that happened in Rincón; very interesting. Sergeant Ochoa was there too. I will pass these around. The other officers you see are from El Condado too. I think we have their names. Hold on a second."

Mayor Ramirez was presenting his information as fast as he could, almost as though the reporters were in a hurry to leave. The truth was that the reporters had never been given so much access to the details of a crime, let alone something that might turn out to be the biggest police cover-up in their memories. Still, Ramirez rushed to unzip the leather pouch he usually carried tucked under his arm, instead of a briefcase. He flipped it open and a bundle of papers fell, spreading themselves out at his feet. He and the deputy mayor knelt to begin picking them up, and Susanna Ortiz stepped to the podium.

"Who are you?" someone shouted out.

"Susanna Ortiz, sheriff of Naranjito. I have more information about this case." She arranged a lock of hair behind her ear and began reading from a steno pad.

"Here is what I have so far," she started. "Sergeant Nestor Ochoa was arrested early this afternoon in Naranjito. He is currently charged with the attempted murder of one of my officers, who he shot while trying to escape apprehension. The officer, whose name I won't release yet, is doing fine. He wore a vest.

"Sergeant Ochoa was, as you know, involved in a bank robbery here, and more details about that are clear now. Seven men took part in the robbery here. There were two police officers and five men released from prison just last night in order to help in this crime. I'll pass out copies of the release forms. Perhaps you can help in deciphering the signatures."

A reporter raised a hand, and Ortiz paused long enough for a question to be shot at her.

"You said there were two policemen involved here. One's in jail. Where's the other?"

"Oh, dead. Sergeant Ochoa shot this suspect in the back of the head in his getaway car. It's my understanding the coroner's office has custody of the body now. His name will be released a bit later."

Sheriff Ortiz went on to explain that the AK-47's had been reported destroyed the year before in the island-wide police effort to keep such weapons from circulating on the streets. The bullet-proof vests were part of a shipment slated to be distributed to a new SWAT team still in the process of being formed.

"But what does any of this have to do with the

Dominicans who came ashore in Rincón?" one of the reporters asked.

"Sheriff Gonzalo was at the beach by coincidence that night. Sergeant Ochoa was there by design. We believe he had something to do with the death of the man you see in the photos being passed around. Sheriff Gonzalo began an investigation into this matter and Sergeant Ochoa wanted to be sure he took Sheriff Gonzalo's focus from what happened on that beach. He had help in getting the men to do this, the weapons and the vests. This will all be disclosed at the trial of Sergeant Ochoa and, I'm sure, the trials of several others. We have already secured several witnesses from the department of corrections and the weapons destruction program. It's only a matter of time before we know everything in detail."

"Do we have a motive for the Rincón murder?" someone called out.

"I'm not prepared to speculate on that right now."

"Is there any idea whether there were people outside of the police who were involved in this?"

"Nothing concrete, but it is something actively being investigated."

"Can a *gandule* arrest a *Metropolitano*?" someone asked half in jest.

The question made Sheriff Ortiz so angry, she had to pause before speaking. While the *Metropolitanos* had been the police of Puerto Rico's major cities for several decades, the state police, commonly called *gandules,* or green beans, because of their drab green uniforms, were a more recent invention and worked mainly in the small towns in Puerto Rico and as a sort of highway patrol. While they carried badges and guns and shared the same duties and rights with the *Metropolitanos,* their brothers in blue, *gandules* were often maligned as mere hick-town cops. The cases they handled tended to be less the sort of thing that appeared on the evening news, more the sort of thing that wound up as town gossip. Yet, only a few hours before, in that very same town, a *gandule* had given her life. In Naranjito, another *gandule* had been shot. If this didn't earn the respect of the reporter, then the man was ignorant.

Sheriff Ortiz walked away from the lectern muttering. Later, an amplified playback of one reporter's audiotape made her words audible: "We have badges, we have guns, we serve, protect, bleed and die too . . ."

Mayor Ramirez took over the conference as Ortiz made her way to a small grocery store less than a block from the plaza.

Ramirez emphasized that Angustias was not a

passive target, and that they would work hard for the conviction of anybody connected to the bank robbery, even if it meant walking into the governor's office with a warrant. "No," he had to explain, "I don't think it would come to that." Then he shrugged. "We'll see."

He also explained what he knew of the attacks on Gonzalo's family and the involvement of the sheriff of Comerio.

"It looks like you know where every sheriff is but your own," someone called out.

Ramirez walked away from the podium and left Jorge Nuñez to handle the dissemination of the photocopies and faxes.

Sheriff Ortiz had bought herself a *Cubano* sandwich and a liter of Coca-Cola and was sitting outside the grocery store in a chair left empty by one of the regular domino players, who had gone to the plaza to see the press conference. From where she sat, she had a view of most of the reporters, and she saw when the conference broke up and the TV journalists began to make their on-camera reports back to the studios.

She finished her sandwich and was balling up the wax paper it had been wrapped in when one of the journalists approached her, casting a shadow over her. He was tall and thin with crisply cut short black hair. His smile showed a perfectly even set of teeth. He was the reporter who had asked about *gandules*.

"I just want to make sure there were no hard feelings about the way I phrased that question." He proffered his right hand, and Ortiz looked at it carefully and decided it wasn't worth shaking.

"One of those *gandules* died today protecting the people of this town. One of my own deputies was shot today. But, hey. Feel free to make fun of people who do a job you will never have the courage to do yourself." She stood up to leave.

"Look. We got off on the wrong foot, here. Can I at least walk you to your car?" he persisted.

"No," she said simply.

He followed her anyway. She wondered if reporters were trained to ignore the requests of the newsworthy.

"Look. Sheriff Ortiz, wait."

She kept walking.

"Sheriff Ortiz, you seem to be the only one in this town that has any clues about what went on here. All I need is to ask a few questions."

Ortiz got to her car and began to open the door, but the reporter put a palm on the door, keeping it closed.

"Listen to me, Sheriff. This is the biggest case of your career. This kind of thing doesn't happen everyday, especially not here. I can put you on

TV; a one-on-one interview. I can guarantee you would be on the evening news tonight, tomorrow, maybe even the next day. You want respect for the officers in green? You want people to know that you guys do as much as anyone else? Then give me an exclusive and every Puerto Rican will know your name and what you do by the end of the day. What do you say, Sheriff?"

Ortiz did not have to think about it.

"I say get your hand off my car. If this were about fame and being on TV, I'd go back to that plaza and get a dozen reporters to listen to me. But it's about murder and warm blood and the death of an officer. Go away before I hurt you." She pulled again on her car door and the reporter let go of it but grabbed her right upper arm instead.

"Then let's go to bed," he said with a sneer. "You've got one hot ass. What do you say?"

She seized his hand with her left hand and gave it a sharp twist outward and back. She used both hands to apply pressure so that the reporter went down on one knee, his wrist brought close now to his ear.

"I say I warned you about getting hurt." And she let him go with a slight push to the asphalt.

On the hillside in La Cola, Gonzalo was failing in his attempt to rush back up the length of rope that had helped him descend. He was exhausted by the day, and no longer had the upper body strength to pull himself up. His left arm was beginning to cramp up on him and his leg with its knee torn open was flexible only with great pain. Also, it was always much harder to fight gravity than go with it, of course. Coming down, a slide of a foot or two was welcome as long as it was controlled. Now that same slide defeated his purpose. After twenty minutes of sweaty struggle, he wondered why he hadn't let the much younger, much stronger Navarro go in his place.

"Estoy cansa'o!" he yelled up to the officers. I'm tired. "I'm going to rest a little," he told them.

He wrapped the nylon cord around his right arm tightly and turned his back on the officers to sit on a rocky outcrop that protruded six or seven inches out of the dirt. He leaned back against the dry, red clay earth. He knew what he wanted from his body. He wanted recuperation in a few minutes' rest. He knew better than that, however. In those few minutes his body would begin to register pains and exhaustions that adrenaline had suppressed. In a few minutes he would feel worse than he already did. In a few minutes he would probably have to give up his climb as well as his pride and ask for help. He was getting old and at the moment he felt as though he had been old for a very long time.

He studied the view from where he sat. He could see all of Naranjito from that height and other towns besides. The mountains of Puerto Rico were more entertaining. They marched away from him, fold after fold, each with its peculiarities—some with tall grass only, some covered densely with trees, some sported a mixture of wild vegetation, others hosted neatly tended farms. One, very distant, appeared to be terraced-off, and Gonzalo was sure he could make out a solitary farmer walking among the terraces. He wondered what it would be like to farm full-time. His father had done that. He knew Collazo had done that before becoming a deputy and would return to doing it until the day he died. Sitting on that hillside with a gentle breeze cooling him after his frustrations, he began to play with the vague idea that he had entertained on and off for many years. He had money saved up. He could farm to supplement his pension. He could read books at night, and sleep well for once, and never see a dead body or look into dead eyes again.

He shook his head sharply to fight off the sleep he was falling into, then the rope twisted around his arm was pulled hard and he was fully awake when he heard his wrist snap. He was on his back, being dragged up the hillside at a phenomenal pace, his right shoulder popped out of its socket. Aside from his initial scream of pain, he made no sound; every time he tried opening his mouth, leaves and blades of grass slapped into it. He grimaced and kept his eyes shut, trying to keep the back of his head off the ground, which was studded with rocks.

As he crested the hill, his body took flight. The picture taken by the photographer showed him nearly three feet off the ground passing the officer in the background at mid-thigh. He landed on asphalt, the back of his head making a loud cracking sound in his ears. The onlookers testified to that sound later, one man saying it sounded like a home run, the photographer saying it sounded like a coconut peeled down to its inner shell being cracked open with a hammer.

Momentum carried him two or three feet on the pavement, tearing open his scalp, ripping through his shirt and undershirt at his shoulder blades and biting into his flesh.

His vision was cloudy with the bright sunlight in his eyes as he saw five of the officers crowd around him and the photographer kneel at his side. The officer with the sunglasses walked to him and bent from the waist to look him in the face.

"You okay?" sunglass man asked.

Gonzalo was about to make some reply: he doesn't remember now what it would have been. No difference. Sunglass man wasn't waiting for an answer. He squatted next to the sheriff and took his right hand into his own and unfurled the nylon rope that was wrapped around it. Then he dropped Gonzalo's arm and walked away.

"Are you okay?" the photographer asked.

She kneeled and put her ear close to his mouth for the response. He said *"Caramba"* hoarsely and fell into unconsciousness. Gonzalo remembers only the darkness that edged into his field of vision and then became all that he could see.

Chapter Nineteen

The six o'clock news on all stations in Puerto Rico was dedicated almost exclusively to the happenings in Angustias. The move by Mayor Ramirez to expose evidence that had not been fully considered was condemned by the governor of the island, by prosecutors and by police officials.

Not that the condemnation mattered to Ramirez. When asked to respond to the governor's charges that he had bungled the case from the beginning, the mayor laughed. "The governor should do his own job and manage the police department of this island. If he did that well, I would have had no trouble today."

Angustias made it through the night without even the hint of further violence. Deputies from both Naranjito and Comerio drove through the hills and valleys of the town and Mayor Ramirez organized a small posse of a half dozen men to do the same.

The next morning did see some more trouble, but it occurred in the town of Naranjito. Sergeant Ochoa had finally been removed to a medical facility in Ponce the evening before and had stayed the night chained to his bed. He was awakened at dawn to prepare for his trip back to Naranjito, where he was to be held until his transfer to San Juan for arraignment. He fell asleep once there, but was awakened again at eight in the morning for a visitor.

The visitor was his lawyer, Pablo Guzman. Guzman was short and very heavy with a belly that spilled over his belt, perhaps the same belt he wore while in college. He was balding though not yet forty years of age. He had known Ochoa for seven years, having helped him in more than a dozen land purchases in Puerto Rico and to fend off two charges of police brutality. Though he was a busy and experienced lawyer, he seemed to everyone in the Naranjito precinct to be lost.

"Can I help you?" he was asked.

"Uh, yeah, sure. Yes, you can. I'm . . . I'm the lawyer for . . . for Nestor Ochoa. I need to speak with him . . . in private. Maybe a conference room. Maybe someplace soundproof, if you have it. Can you do that for me?"

"Sure thing. Just wait right over there; we'll transfer him to conference room number two. That's on the second floor. When he's ready, someone will escort you up, all right?"

"Sure, sure."

Guzman sat on the plastic chair pointed out to him and took out a handkerchief to wipe the sweat forming at his eyebrow. From where he sat he had a clear view of his client hobbled by hog-tie chains and a beige and blue hard plastic leg brace that kept him from flexing his torn thigh muscle. He watched Ochoa through the corner of his eye, not wanting to make eye contact until they were both in the conference room.

Ochoa never looked at him. Instead, he kept his eyes on the floor, grimacing from the pain of each step. He had a thick beard growing already. His hair was disordered, and Guzman knew he smelled. Ochoa always seemed to have a peculiar and bad smell to him.

A minute later, an officer came to escort Guzman to conference room number two. He labored up the stairs as slowly as Ochoa had done, a briefcase tucked under his arm, his free hand on the handrail, helping to pull his weight up the stairs.

"Okay, this room is soundproof. There is recording equipment if you want . . ."

"No, I have my own, thanks."

The officer opened the door to the room and showed Guzman in. Ochoa was already seated and restrained. He was smoking a cigarette and nodded to Guzman as the man walked in.

"Smoking's allowed in here?" Guzman asked.

Of course, many rooms of this type were officially smoke-free, but detectives frequently smoked in them. It was a small annoyance to some prisoners and a reward to others.

"Well, the sprinklers haven't worked in years, so, yes, I guess smoking is allowed. If you want me to remove the cigarette from the prisoner . . ."

"No, no."

"And the restraints?" the officer asked.

"The restraints? Oh, the handcuffs and all that? Uh, . . . no." He whispered the final word as though Ochoa would not be able to figure out that Guzman thought him dangerous and didn't want him loose in the room.

"Well, when you want out of here, just press this buzzer." He pointed to a spot on the wall near the door. "It rings downstairs and I'll be a minute in getting to you. Just ring once, okay? It's loud enough downstairs."

The officer locked the door, and Guzman set his briefcase on the table. Ochoa took another long drag of his cigarette before speaking.

"What? Aren't you even going to say 'hello' to

your star client? Better go on a diet. I'm gonna put you on TV, *gordito*."

Guzman pulled out his chair and sat, saying nothing to the insult. He opened his briefcase and started rummaging through it, shuffling papers.

"You know what they told me this morning?" Ochoa continued. "They said, 'Wake up. Your lawyer's here.' I said, 'I didn't ask for a lawyer. What's his name? Is he a great big fat guy? Does his belly cover up his *pinga?*' I tell you the deputy laughed. I guess I can describe a guy, can't I?"

Guzman ignored these insults too and looked up at his client. Ochoa took another long drag of his cigarette and flicked ashes onto the table.

"Well, my little *lechóncito*, what have you got for me? Did you bring me a file? Maybe you've got the keys to this place. What do you have? Good news, I hope."

Guzman opened his mouth and closed it again. He clearly had no idea where to begin. Ochoa laughed; he knew Guzman was seriously out of his depth with a case of this magnitude and importance. Still, he would do for now until all the charges were formalized against him. So far, he had only been charged with the attempted murder of a Naranjito deputy. He knew that was bound to change, probably even that same day.

"Well? Don't just waste my time here. Talk already," Ochoa insisted.

"I want you to know I don't want to do this," Guzman said.

"I know that. Any lawyer who wants to deal with my case has to be either crazy or have huge balls made out of steel. You're not crazy, and I bet you haven't seen yours since grade school. But what have you got for me? What's your first move?"

"I want you to know I don't want to do this, but they have my daughter, Ochoa. She's only six years old. I need to get her back. You understand me?"

Ochoa took the cigarette from his lips. "Shit," he said. "You're gonna shoot me?"

"I have to do what they say. You know how they are. They took her last night. I had her in my arms, they put a gun to her head, I let her go. What was I supposed to do? I have to do it. You see how it is?" Guzman asked.

"Think, fatboy. How far do you think you're going to get? Think. You think the people I work for are going to let your girl get out of this alive? You think you're going to survive this? Trust me, I'm your only hope. Get me out of here, and I can get your girl for you. Believe me."

"I'm sorry."

Guzman pulled a kerosene squeeze bottle from his briefcase and began spraying Ochoa's clothes. Ochoa began to scream, but Guzman sprayed into his mouth, shutting it. He doused his client's hair and the chair Ochoa was trying to get out of. The chair toppled over, and Ochoa hit the floor squirming to get free. Guzman kneeled next him with a cigarette lighter.

"Sorry. I had to. You understand," he said, then he flicked open the lighter and touched the flame to Ochoa's hair and shirt and pants.

The sergeant screamed in pain. Guzman stood up and backed away as the flames began to grow. He capped the kerosene bottle and put it in his briefcase as the smell of burning hair and flesh began to fill the room. He picked up his briefcase, tucked it under his arm and pressed the buzzer a half dozen times frantically. He pounded on the door. This was part of the planned act, but it was also sincere. The room was beginning to fill with black smoke as the plastic chair and the plastic leg brace began to burn. He rang the buzzer again, and the door opened.

"He's on fire! He's on fire! Get an extinguisher!" Guzman yelled.

Three officers rushed into the room. One of them tried to pull Ochoa out of the room by his leg restraints, but they were searing hot to the touch. Another officer ripped off his own shirt and tried to beat the flames down, but it caught fire itself and had to be tossed on the floor and stamped on. In the hallway, a half dozen other officers were rushing toward the room with blankets, buckets of sand and an extinguisher. Government workers from other offices were rushing out of the building. Guzman walked quickly in the flow of clerks and accountants, other lawyers and their secretaries. In fact, when he reached the first floor, he was walking shoulder to shoulder with a deputy mayor of Naranjito.

Outside, Guzman headed straight for his car. He stopped when one of the women who had just evacuated the building screamed and pointed at him. He turned a full three hundred and sixty degrees before realizing that she was pointing at the sleeve of his jacket. It was on fire, and he whipped it off and threw it to the ground, stepping on it until the small flame was out. Then he put it back on, got in his car and drove away to a roadside pay phone near San Juan. He waited there all day and into the night for a call about his daughter, which never came.

The channel seven news interrupted a daytime quiz show to report the news of the attack on Ochoa, and Gonzalo watched the special report from his bed in the Angustias clinic. Mari was at his side, about to give her husband an update on his mother's medical condition, when she was preempted as well.

Ochoa was near death with burns over nearly sixty percent of his body. The announcer seemed amazed that his nose had been burned off as well as his lips. She reported that he had lost an eye in the attack as well as a total of three fingers. His own lawyer was being sought for questioning though it was known that the sergeant was smoking when last seen before the fire. A picture of the lawyer's pudgy face was put on the screen and the man smiled to his audience.

"Do you think he'll die?" Mari asked.

"Yep. That lawyer doesn't stand a chance. He doesn't know the people he's playing with," Gonzalo answered.

"I meant Ochoa."

"Ochoa? Never. The devil has a use for him, I'm sure."

Gonzalo used the remote control to lower the volume on the television. He turned his attention to his wife.

"What was it you were going to say?"

"I was going to tell you about your mother. She's not well, Gonzalo."

"What do you mean she's not well? What does that mean?"

"I mean she had a stroke. She's . . ."

"A stroke?"

"The guys who tied her up did nothing to her. It was the scare. She had a stroke, a bad one."

"Is she going to die?"

"No. Well, I mean, not immediately. She'll survive this stroke, but she won't be the same as before. She—"

"Not the same as before what? Before the stroke or when she was young?"

"Let me just tell you the information I have, okay? Look. She's paralyzed. There's no good way to explain this. She won't walk again. She will need training to talk again. Maybe six months. Luis, her right side is dead, lifeless. It might get a little better, a little. For now, she can't feed herself, go to the bathroom by herself. I don't know. The doctors said a lot of things."

"I've got to get to her," Gonzalo said, and made a motion to raise himself from the bed.

"She's not going to die," Mari said, trying to push her husband back to bed gently.

"She's in a hospital alone. No one to visit her. She'll be afraid."

"She spends most of her time asleep. She doesn't remember anyone yet. The doctors say her memory will return in the next few days."

"I'm not going just for her sake, Mari. I need to be there. What kind of a son wouldn't go?"

"Okay, okay. I'll check you out of here. I'll drive you over, but I want to talk for a minute first. Please, just lie back. Thank you. Now, your mother is going to need constant care when she gets home. The doctors said she won't be able to do very much for herself—"

"Between you and I we can—"

"No. No, Luis. She needs someone there living with her. We have a seven-year-old daughter. We can only do so much. Do you understand me? We need to find her a nurse who can live in with her."

"How long will she be in the hospital?"

"No one was sure about that. Nobody gave me an estimate that was less than two weeks. Most of the doctors talked about two months or more. She needs intensive physical therapy just to learn how to say 'yes' and 'no'."

Gonzalo sat still for a moment but was soon trying to get out of his bed again.

"I need to see her," he said, and he forced his way out of bed.

His right hand was in a plaster cast and his right arm was in a sling. His head had a bandage all the way around it, and he walked with a limp because he was trying to keep his shoulders from moving.

"We'll go to see your mother. I'm not saying no, but I have to talk to you about something before we see her, okay? I want to make sure we tell her the same thing."

"What are we going to tell her?" Gonzalo paused with only one leg in his pants.

"I got a call this morning, before I got here."

"From who?"

"From your sister."

"From Rosita?" Gonzalo asked with his eyes opened wide now.

"That's her. She called at six in the morning."

"She was awake at six in the morning?" That was an even greater surprise.

"Well, she was calling from Spain."

"Spain?"

"Spain. It's later over there. Anyway. Angustias is in the news everywhere. America knows all about what happened here, and apparently it was on the news in Spain. When she heard something about Puerto Rico, she paid attention. She says she was shocked to see Angustias on TV. I believe her."

"Well . . . that's okay. I'll tell Mama—"

"Rosita's coming back to Puerto Rico. She called from the airport in Madrid. Said she was waiting for her flight."

"Did she call collect?"

"Yes."

"Okay. Just checking to make sure it was her. Go on. What does she want?"

"I told her about your mother. She said she was coming to help. That's all I wanted to tell you about. She's planning to live in your mother's house. She'll be Sonia's nurse."

"No. She won't. She's irresponsible. She walked away from us . . . I don't even know how long ago."

"So you're going to keep her away from your mother? Your mother who has lighted a candle for her every week for decades? Now she wants to return, but you're deciding not to let her? Think about it, Luis."

"I have thought about it. A million times."

"And all you can come up with is bitterness? Revenge? That's the best you can do? Look. It's not my place. I don't really know Rosita. But I think you can do better than that. Forgive her, Luis. For your sake."

Gonzalo finished putting on his clothes and thought about the request that was being made of him. He wondered when it was that his wife became wiser than he, and decided to leave that question alone since the answer might very well be that she had started out wiser.

"If she screws up again, there will be no forgiveness," he finally said.

"I didn't say there should be," Mari answered.

* * *

Rosita Gonzalo's airplane landed at Luis Muñoz Marin International Airport in San Juan at three in the afternoon. She was back on her homeland for the first time in . . . she didn't know how many years. For reasons she well understood, there was no one at the airport to greet her, and she got her own bags. She took a hired car, a *carro público*, from the airport to her mother's hospital in Ponce.

In the room, she saw Gonzalo first, standing next to a woman who was far older than the mother she had last seen. She nearly excused herself and walked out because the picture of Gonzalo shown in the Spanish media showed him healthy, standing behind Mayor Ramirez in a press conference. Also, her brother had been thin. Gonzalo was beginning to put on weight.

"You're in the right room, Rosita," Gonzalo called to her. "Come see your mother."

There are times when healing is a simple thing. The aggrieved may be disposed to forgiveness. Those who realize they have done wrong may be willing to be forgiven. On this day, Gonzalo, who had often claimed to hate his sister though he hadn't even seen her in a decade, was too tired to fight; he had no stomach for it and preferred harmony instead. Rosita, who had in that same decade resented her brother's judgment of her, was sapped of all power to defend herself. She wanted only to be at her mother's side, to feel herself a part of a family again. Brother and sister were therefore able to pick up their relationship, going back to a time before hating each other, a time when they were friends and loved each other. Decades, that day, were erased.

Epilogue

Nestor Ochoa survived his burns. He spent six months in New York University Hospital's burn unit recuperating and being reconstructed. At the end of that time, he was remanded back to the Puerto Rican judicial system. He pled guilty to all charges related to the bank robbery and the attempted murder of the officer in Naranjito, but claimed against the photographic evidence that he had never been in Rincón. He knew nothing of any conspiracy except the one to rob the bank. The robbery was not intended to distract Sheriff Gonzalo from any investigation he might be carrying out; it was intended, like most robberies, to gain money.

For those crimes he pled guilty to, he was sentenced to sixty years of prison time. He served three days before he was found at morning roll call still resting calmly under his covers with a sharpened screwdriver rammed in his ear. There was only a very lazy investigation, and his killer was never found.

The trials and investigations surrounding Ochoa's actions on Las Puntas ended two years after his death with the arrest and conviction of nine members of the police department—six beat cops, one sergeant, one lieutenant and one commander. Ochoa's captain at the El Condado precinct was relieved of his command and retired. The judge who signed the release forms for the ex-cons who helped in the bank robbery was "asked" by the governor to retire, and he did.

The case was taken no further. The police and the governor's office were satisfied. Almost everyone else on the island knew there had to be more to the case than a few low-level policemen and a judge. Every day people speculated that a hammer was going to be brought down on police corruption, ridding the department of a few captains, a few deputy chiefs, possibly even the chief of police; but the hammer blow never came.

For a year or two there was a greater vigilance on the West Coast of Puerto Rico by the U.S. Coast Guard. But this subsided, and small craft still occasionally make their way onto the rocks at Las Puntas, and occasionally there is the suspicion that they were forced onto the rocks on purpose. For many desperate Dominicans, death is a consequence of chasing the American Dream.

One relationship was broken by the work of Sergeant Ochoa. Emilio Collazo refused to come back to work for the police department. He was seventy-seven years old, and his wife was convinced he was too old for the job. Besides, he had a farm that was covered with weeds and tall grass for the most part. He had no financial need for the job, and his wife Cristina wanted him at home.

"Is it the fact that you killed a man?" Gonzalo asked. They were sitting on rocking chairs on Collazo's porch.

"Death doesn't impress me like it used to, son. I found my own father dead when I was eight years old. I don't know how many people I've seen dead.

"Look at Hector. He can break his ribs and be back at work in a week. He's a young man, strong, with perfect vision. He's the man for you," Collazo said.

"Are you worried about not being able to do your job? I can tell you—"

"Listen to me, son. If Rosa Almodovar had Hector as her partner, she would be alive today. Am I right or am I wrong?"

"I can't tell you—"

"Am I right?" Collazo insisted.

"Possibly, but—"

"Let me tell you. There is no doubt in my mind Hector or you even would have put that bastard, excuse me, that bastard on the ground. Rosa would be alive. It's not death that bothers me. I'd shoot the man who killed Rosa a thousand times if I had to. I didn't confess shooting him. I'm proud of it. It was just too late, that's all. I was too slow, that's all. Well, I won't be slow again."

The two men rocked in silence for a minute longer, then Gonzalo rose and extended his hand to Collazo, who took it.

"The city is grateful for your years of service. I am proud to call you friend still. If you need anything of me, you know where I am. I'll bring your paperwork at the end of the week."

With that, the first deputy Gonzalo had ever hired was discharged from the force. He continues to farm his land to this day and has recently added two acres to the seventeen he has cared for.

The photographer from Las Puntas decided to make a home in Angustias. She survived the crash that destroyed her car because she wasn't in the car when it was hit. She had come to a screeching halt at the end of the road in La Cola. The car she had been avoiding for most of an hour that night came around the final curve only a second or two after she had grabbed her bag and jumped out of the car and into the overgrown weeds in

front of an abandoned house. The car chasing her
(probably a Cadillac, she thinks) never slowed
down. It rammed her Mitsubishi from behind,
then reversed its way out of La Cola. She spent
the night in a closet of the house, which she later
bought from the city of Angustias for almost
nothing. She wanted a quiet place for writing and
there may be no quieter place on the island.

Lucy Aponte had grown up in the not-so-far-
away town of Ciales, but had gone to New York
on a scholarship to study journalism at Colum-
bia. She quit after two years of study and tried
getting a job with the newspapers in Puerto Rico,
but each of them reviewed her resume and were
sorry they had no need for a person with her exact qualifications. Her photos of the carnage on
Las Puntas and an accompanying story she wrote
were sold to the *New Yorker* and considered for a
Pulitzer. She wrote another article on the trail of
police and official corruption in Puerto Rico that
was sold to the *Atlantic*. She felt herself set for the
career she wanted.

"But you should be in New York or at least San
Juan, if you want to be a journalist," Gonzalo
warned her.

"Why? I have a camera, a fax machine, and a
computer. I'm not on Mars. If I need to go to San
Juan, I'll drive. The city is extending the electric

lines up there. I have two five-hundred-gallon water tanks and a filter. I don't need much else."

In Santo Domingo, in the fishing village of Ramona, Isabel Montez waited for her husband to come back from the sea. She told reporters that he had two hundred and fifty dollars of American money in his pockets as his pay for piloting the ship. She remains convinced that the outturned pockets prove he was killed for this cash. She raises her daughter alone still, taking odd jobs and surviving on the charity of others. Her husband's body was never really looked for in Puerto Rico and never found.

DAVID LAWRENCE

NOTHING LIKE THE NIGHT

Once she had been beautiful. Now she was eight days dead. Janice Parker had been young and glamorous, living with a roommate in a fancy Notting Hill apartment. Now Janice has been found murdered—stabbed fifty times—and her roommate is missing. Assigned to the case is Detective Stella Mooney, smart and tough, but maybe just a little fragile underneath. Soon the evidence suggests that she and her team are facing a very special and terrifying killer, one who hunts his prey to satisfy a never-ending desire. But Stella keeps digging, and as the case gradually unfolds she comes to realize that the truth may be more shocking than she ever suspected.

- -

THE JULIAN SECRET

GREGG LOOMIS

Don Huff was Lang Reilly's friend, and now he's been brutally murdered. Could someone be willing to commit murder to prevent the book he was writing from ever seeing the light of day? What secrets are worth killing for? Lang is determined to find the truth, but the organization that killed his friend is just as eager to kill him if he gets too close.

The trail of secrets leads Lang on a deadly chase across Europe, deeper and deeper into a mystery that has been concealed since the days of the founding of the Catholic Church. Danger follows Lang with every startling revelation. But at the end of the hunt lies a final secret that will shock even Lang—if he survives long enough to find it!

- -

R. BARRI FLOWERS

STATE'S EVIDENCE

Assistant District Attorney Beverly Mendoza has been selected to prosecute a disturbing case: the murder of a judge and the rape of his wife. The defendant, Rafael Santiago, once vowed to get revenge against the judge and his wife. It seems like an open-and-shut case. But appearances can be very deceiving.

At the same time, detective Stone Palmer is investigating the rape and strangling of a young woman. Career criminal Manuel Gonzalez is in custody, but he pulls the rug out from everyone when he claims he's the one who murdered the judge. Could it be a case of mistaken identity? Or two desperate, violent men out to manipulate and beat the system?

- -

JEFF BUICK
AFRICAN
ICE

A diamond formation worth untold millions, hidden deep in the jungles of Africa. Many have tried—and failed—to find it. Can Samantha Carlson do the impossible? The president of Gem-Star thinks so when he hires the geologist to lead a team into the Democratic Republic of Congo and return with the diamonds' location.

Samantha is aware the odds are against her from the beginning, but she knows what she's doing. Plus, Gem-Star has provided an escort team to protect her. But Samantha's expedition is about to turn into an all-out battle for survival. There's another team on a mission in the jungle. Their goal: kill Samantha.

ANDREW COBURN

ON THE LOOSE

By the time he was twelve years old, young Bobby Sawhill had killed two people, brutally and with no remorse. He was tried as a juvenile and sentenced to a youth detention center, where he refused counseling. All he seems to care about is bodybuilding, getting bigger. Stronger. Soon he'll be twenty-one. He'll be released— and then Bobby's coming home. Home to a small town that will live in fear, certain that Bobby will kill again, unable to do anything but wait for him to strike.
